THE

FOLD

AN
NA

THE

FOLD

G. P. PUTNAM'S SONS

G. P. PUTNAM'S SONS
A division of Penguin Young Readers Group.
Published by The Penguin Group.
Penguin Group (USA) Inc., 375 Hudson Street, New York, NY 10014, U.S.A. Penguin Group (Canada), 90 Eglinton Avenue East, Suite 700, Toronto, Ontario M4P 2Y3, Canada (a division of Pearson Penguin Canada Inc.). Penguin Books Ltd, 80 Strand, London WC2R 0RL, England. Penguin Ireland, 25 St. Stephen's Green, Dublin 2, Ireland (a division of Penguin Books Ltd.). Penguin Group (Australia), 250 Camberwell Road, Camberwell, Victoria 3124, Australia (a division of Pearson Australia Group Pty Ltd). Penguin Books India Pvt Ltd, 11 Community Centre, Panchsheel Park, New Delhi–110 017, India. Penguin Group (NZ), 67 Apollo Drive, Rosedale, North Shore 0632, New Zealand (a division of Pearson New Zealand Ltd.). Penguin Books (South Africa) (Pty) Ltd, 24 Sturdee Avenue, Rosebank, Johannesburg 2196, South Africa. Penguin Books Ltd, Registered Offices: 80 Strand, London WC2R 0RL, England.

Published simultaneously in Canada.
Printed in the United States of America.
Book design by Richard Amari.
Text set in Apollo.

Library of Congress Cataloging-in-Publication Data
An, Na. The fold / An Na. p. cm.
Summary: Korean American high school student Joyce Kim feels like a nonentity compared to her beautiful older sister, and when her aunt offers to pay for plastic surgery on her eyes, she jumps at the chance, thinking it will change her life for the better. 1. Korean Americans—Juvenile fiction. [1. Korean Americans—Fiction. 2. Beauty, Personal—Fiction. 3. Identity—Fiction. 4. Interpersonal relations—Fiction. 5. Self-confidence—Fiction.] I. Title. PZ7.A51822Fo 2008 [Fic]—dc22   2007019420   ISBN 978-0-399-24276-2
1 3 5 7 9 10 8 6 4 2

For Juna and James
Who love me faults and all

THE

FOLD

joyce stared at herself in the mirror, twisting her head from side to side, finger combing more of her long black hair over the unsightly bulge that used to be her temple. What had started as a tiny red bump had swollen and grown in circumference with each passing hour and day, building up over the week into a massive burial mound on the side of her head. And though Joyce had tried to head it off with her arsenal of tools and tricks accumulated over years of poring through beauty magazines, the medication, steaming and "gentle" squeezing did nothing to stop the growth.

"Joyce, we're really leaving now." Helen, her older sister, banged on the locked bathroom door.

"Okay, okay. I'll be right out."

Joyce stepped away from the mirror and turned to reach for the doorknob, but a flash of redness drew her eyes once more. She grunted in disgust. It was no use. She had to do it. She had to go in again.

Joyce stepped back to the mirror and pulled out two sheets of tissue from the dispenser on the counter. She leaned forward, raising her tissue-swathed index fingers to her face. The huge zit pulsed with pain, but she held her breath and gave it. One. Last. Push. Eye-rolling, teeth-clenching, nausea-inducing, searing pain flooded her body, but in the mirror, Joyce could see the beginnings of a white nugget like a tiny grain of rice oozing out from under her skin along with pus-streaked blood. Joyce gasped and watched with revolt and glee as the alien seed emerged from the mother ship that was her temple. She got it.

Joyce leaned over the sink, dizzy from the pain. The last day of school and Joyce was still in no shape to ask John Ford Kang to sign her yearbook. But this was it. There would be no other chances. Her upcoming senior year depended on this moment.

Joyce checked her face in the mirror. She was still deformed, but at least now, with the blockage out, the zit might deflate by the end of fifth period. Joyce pressed the tissue paper to her temple and grimaced in pain. Please, please go down.

While she waited for her zit to stop oozing, Joyce paced around the small bathroom and practiced her line for John.

"Hey, John, do me a favor and sign my yearbook?

"Lame," she said and stared at the tile floor. "Hi, John. Sign this for me."

Joyce reached for her tube of Extra Strength Zap Zit and dabbed it around the opening of the pimple, which was red and ragged, puckered dead from all the picking. The sting of the medication made her eyes tear up, but this was proof that it was working. Joyce stared at her face, hoping now her reflection would let her go. But it was no use. The Thanksgiving cranberry of a zit glistened with a medicinal shine. She was Rudolph with a misplaced nose. A cheese pizza with a renegade pepperoni. Joyce clamped her hand over it. The thing needed to be hidden away.

Joyce pulled out the drawer and reached for her heavy-duty concealer makeup stick. She dotted the perimeter of the zit with the beige marker and then tried to blend it in with her fingertip. The redness was toned down, but no amount of makeup could hide the rawness of the skin around the lesion. Joyce's shoulders slumped forward. What was the use? She might as well draw a line down the middle of her face. Quasimodo on this side. Plain Korean girl on this side. Joyce could see the tears welling up again in her reflection. Nothing was going to work.

Stop obsessing, she told herself. You'll be late for school. Joyce pulled more of her hair forward, using it like a dark curtain cutting short a bad performance. Stay under, she told it, and finally stepped away from the mirror.

Joyce rushed out of the bathroom and into the living room. Where were Helen and Andy? Had she heard the door slam? As Joyce grabbed her backpack off the couch, a note on the coffee table caught her eye. Helen's handwriting.

Joyce grabbed the note. Her eyes flicked back and forth as she quickly scanned the words.

"HELEN!" Joyce screamed into the empty apartment. She heaved her backpack to the floor and crumpled the note in her hand. Joyce ran back to her room and searched the top of her dresser for the key to the lock on her bike. This was just like Helen. Everything had to revolve around her schedule. Helen was going to be late and she had to drop off Andy, their younger brother, at school. Helen had a meeting, so Joyce could ride her bike. Joyce flung a stack of paper to the floor and found the key. She snatched it up and ran out of the apartment, slamming the door behind her.

The whole reason Joyce had asked for a ride in the first place was that today was not just some ordinary day. And if Helen had even taken a millisecond to think about anybody else besides herself, then maybe she would have noticed how hard Joyce had been trying to look good today.

Joyce pedaled furiously, the bright morning sun glaring into her eyes as she rode out of the apartment complex and onto the streets. As she started her ascent up the hill to her high school, beads of sweat popped up on her forehead. Damn this heat. Damn this sweat. Damn you, Helen. Oh, God. Joyce quickly reached up to her zit. Same size. Well, at least it's not bigger, she thought.

Even though Helen was heading into her second year of college, she still lived at home and used the family sedan like it was her own. Joyce had gotten her driver's license over six months ago, but she rarely had the chance to drive. Once Helen didn't have to get to classes every day, Joyce vowed to herself that it would be her turn to get the car.

Joyce crested the top of the hill, and the city of Orangedale spread out below her. The heavy freeway traffic of Southern California crept along as the morning commuters sat in their cars talking on their cell phones and inching their way to work. And if she squinted just so, Joyce could imagine that she saw a ribbon of the Pacific Ocean glimmering in the distance.

Joyce coasted down the hill, past the line of cars headed into the parking lot of her high school, and stopped at the bike rack. All around her, there was an upbeat intensity to everyone's steps and chatter. The last day of school felt almost as good as the first day of summer. Joyce jumped off her bike. This summer was going to be completely different, and it would all start with doing something that she had dreamed of all year long.

John Ford Kang. She was finally going to talk to him. She was going to say something witty to make him laugh. Maybe a joke about school. And then John would laugh and sign her yearbook while she signed his. Joyce had the perfect phrase: Make every minute count. So what if Joyce had stolen it from a greeting card—John would never know. And then over the summer, he would look at her clever note and remember talking to her. Joyce had it all planned out.

Leave him curious, and at the start of senior year, she would walk into school and knock him over with her transformation. She was going to wash her face every night and exercise to get rid of her fatty knees so she could wear short skirts. And come fall, when she walked into Orangedale with her clear complexion, stylish new haircut and sexy clothes, John would fall to his knees. Joyce smiled. Well, she would settle for just a little drool.

Some girls in the distance were squealing and hugging as though they were never going to see each other again. Probably seniors being melodramatic, like they didn't have all summer to go to the mall or hang out on the beach. Joyce still had one more year, and that year was going to count, not like all her other high school days that blurred into one long yawn. Joyce took a deep breath and exhaled her nervousness as she reached up to remove her backpack. In that second, right as her hand pawed her empty shoulder, she slammed into a wall of realization. Her mind's eye traveled back across the streets, back into her apartment, to the living room floor next to the crumpled note.

"HELEN!"

A few students glanced over. Joyce quickly knelt down and pretended to be busy locking up her bike.

She pressed the heel of her palms to her damp eyes and tried not to linger on thoughts of a bad omen. Signs. This was turning into one of those days.

"Stop it," she whispered. Joyce finger combed more of her hair over her zit and forced herself to stand up. She would just buy another yearbook. There was nothing wrong with that. The plan would still work. It wasn't a big deal. And yet, the negative thoughts lingered. Too many things going wrong. Maybe this wasn't a good day to ask John to sign her yearbook? Joyce gulped back her reservations. No. This was it. There were no other chances. No such thing as bad omens, Joyce tried to convince herself.

Joyce slowly walked toward her English classroom, her eyes lasered onto a figure in the distance. John Ford Kang stood with his buddies two doors down the hall, their backpacks thrown in the middle of their circle. He towered over his blond surfer friends, his frame tall and muscular, unlike so many other stringbean Korean guys. But then, he was only half Korean and half something else. Dutch or German or something else, exotic, European. His mother had been a model, it was rumored. Joyce's arms felt uncomfortably empty without the weight of her backpack on one shoulder. She crossed her arms in front of her, but then thought they looked too weird that way. Would he look at her, she wondered, burying her hands in the front pockets of her jeans. Look at me, she whispered in her head. Look at me. Look at me. Her zit throbbed. No, don't look at me.

He cut one hand through the air, his head bobbing to emphasize some point he was making. He was so close, Joyce had the urge to walk right over and touch his shoulder. Turn his perfect face toward her so she could gaze up into his eyes, which she had overheard other girls talking about as this amazing light shade of brown rimmed with green. She had never been that close to him, but she could imagine. And had imagined many days and nights as she thought about ways to talk to him. Thought about how to get him to fall in love with her.

"Come on, stalker." Gina prodded Joyce to move along. "Where's your backpack?"

Joyce blinked rapidly as though she had been staring at the sun too long and then smiled at her best friend. "Long story, but I can say one word. Helen."

Gina groaned sympathetically and they linked arms before heading into their English classroom.

at lunchtime, Gina and Joyce headed over to their usual bench under the eucalyptus tree in the central quad. Not many people ventured near the "death tree" as everyone called it because the eucalyptus shed its branches, twigs and bark on a regular basis, forming a ring of debris. But it also meant that the bench was empty at peak quad times when the "beautiful people" usually took their choice spots at the other benches. Gina and Joyce found that sitting close to the trunk reduced the number of things they had to pick out of their hair after watching their reality show that was Orangedale High at lunch.

Gina brushed off the bench before sitting down and then opened up her container of yogurt. She craned her neck to see past the tall basketball players chatting up two of the cheerleaders.

"Oh, no," Gina cried. "I can't believe Bill Newsom is still talking to Jenny Perry after she hooked up with his best friend at prom. That is so sick. But then again, Jenny does look hot in that dress."

Joyce smiled down at her friend, who was impeccably groomed as always. While Gina and Joyce were similarly dressed in jeans and T-shirts, Gina knew how to go that extra step, with a nice belt here and a silver necklace there, so that Gina looked put together whereas Joyce felt like she barely hung together.

Joyce glanced over at the group, but for once, she had no interest in what they were doing. She was too worried about what she had to do.

"I don't care what Jenny's wearing. I need another yearbook."

Gina kept her eyes on the group and stirred her yogurt. "Joyce, you can't just buy another yearbook."

"Oh, right, I'm gonna go up to him and ask him to sign a piece of paper like some stalkerazzi." Joyce peeled the wrapper off her candy bar and took a large bite. She savored the chocolate, letting it melt on her tongue. "I have ten bucks, so will you lend me forty? I have the money at home."

"You are a stalker, don't even try and deny. But come on, Joyce! Fifty dollars!" Gina pointed her spoon at Joyce. "Do you know what you can buy for fifty dollars?"

"Yeah. A new yearbook."

Gina shook her head and lifted a tiny spoonful of yogurt to her lips. This had become their lunchtime routine. Gina pretending to eat her yogurt while Joyce ate her chocolate.

"You shouldn't eat chocolate, you know. Gives you zits," Gina said.

Joyce took another bite of the candy bar and then lifted back the hair covering her temple.

"Ahh!" Gina gasped. "What did you do to yourself?"

"This chocolate bar can't give me zits. I already have one."

"Sicko, that's like smoking when you have lung cancer," Gina said.

Joyce shrugged and popped the last bit of the chocolate bar into her mouth. Gina watched with envy. It had been almost three months since Gina had sworn off junk food, and to Joyce's surprise, Gina had held firm, already losing five pounds, but none of it from her face, which was where she had hoped it would disappear. After being called Moon Pie by one of her mom's friends, Gina couldn't stop obsessing about her large cheeks. Joyce thought Gina's soft, round face made her look cute. Gina thought it made her look like a Japanese cartoon character. Sometimes, if Joyce was in a bad mood, Gina would pull a baseball cap over her hair and point into the distance saying with a bad Japanese accent, "Look! It's Godzilla!"

Joyce and Gina had been best friends ever since Gina's mom came to work at the Korean restaurant that Joyce's family owned. Gina was short for Eugenia, a name Gina hated as much as Joyce hated her name, but at least Gina got a cool nickname out of the deal, whereas there was nothing Joyce could do to shorten her name to something respectable. Joy was about it, but it made Joyce worry that someone would break out singing a Christmas carol. For one week in the fourth grade, she had tried to get everyone to call her Joey, but then Jimmy Lee started saying it with a deep mafia accent, drawing out the *e*, and Joyce gave up being Joeeeeeey.

"A new swimsuit," Gina said.

"What?" Joyce stood up to throw away her candy bar wrapper.

"Fifty bucks would buy you a new swimsuit for the

summer." Gina grimaced and finally forced down a bite of yogurt.

"I don't need a new swimsuit. I need a yearbook." Joyce remained standing. "Are you coming or not?"

Gina looked down at her yogurt. With a sigh, she stood up and dumped the container in the trash. "Come on, stalker, let's go to the bookstore. I need a granola bar anyway."

They walked to a large building at the far end of the quad that housed the student government offices and the bookstore/snack shop that the organization ran for fund-raising. Gina and Joyce pushed their way past a sea of natural and artificial blond hair. The store was always packed, even though most of the people weren't there to buy anything. At least not anything legal. It was just a place to go. A place to meet. A place to be seen.

Gina went to the side of the store where they sold snacks, and Joyce pushed her way past the bodies to the back register and stood in line. All along the walls there were framed pictures of past student government officers. Joyce tried not to glance up at the picture of Helen, the first and only Asian American female president of Orangedale. Even though Helen had graduated over a year ago, Joyce was reminded of

Helen's legacy at every display case that housed med-
als and plaques.

Joyce turned her back on the picture of Helen as
she waited for her turn in line and scanned the heads,
looking for anyone dark haired. Anyone tall and dark
haired with reportedly beautiful brown-green eyes.

"Hey, move up, it's your turn," a heavily muscled
guy in a white T-shirt said.

Joyce turned back in line and stepped forward.

"I need a yearbook," she said.

The student behind the counter turned around and
reached into a full box and pulled out a silver and blue
yearbook.

"Fifty," he said drumming his fingers on the counter.

Joyce reached into her pocket and pulled out a ten.
She looked over her shoulder for Gina, who was still
standing in front of the snack display.

"Gina," Joyce called, "I need the money."

The muscle guy started to complain loudly. "Jesus
Christ, would you get moving?"

Joyce started feeling anxious and yelled louder.
"GINA!"

Gina waved her finger for one more second.

"Jesus, you Oriental bitches move as slow as you
drive," muscle guy muttered.

Joyce pretended not to hear and fidgeted with her hair, tucking it back behind her ears.

Gina finally tapped her shoulder and handed her one five and two twenty-dollar bills and a granola bar packet.

"Took you long enough," muscle guy said.

Gina shot him an annoyed look.

Joyce quickly threw down the money and grabbed the yearbook. As the student behind the counter started to hand Joyce the change, she caught him staring at the side of her head. Joyce could feel the egg pulsing with attention. She quickly grabbed the change and ran out of the bookstore.

"Joyce, wait up," Gina called.

Joyce cleared the crowd and finally stopped in the hallway. Gina caught up to her.

"What's wrong with you?"

"I hate this place," Joyce said, staring down the empty hall, clutching the yearbook to her chest.

Gina pulled the edge of the yearbook down and grabbed the granola bar and her change from Joyce.

"What's new?" Gina said, peeling open the wrapper of her granola bar. They started walking down the hall. "Come on. It's the last day of school. You're supposed to be happy."

Joyce laughed bitterly. "Yeah, right. I just paid fifty dollars for a second yearbook and got called an Oriental bitch by that meathead in the bookstore. And then the guy behind the counter was staring at my zit. Did you see him?"

Gina stopped. "What did that jerk call you?"

"Us. He called us Oriental bitches who move as slow as we drive."

Gina closed her eyes and bit down on her lower lip. Then she opened her eyes and let loose. "That jock-grabbing, ass-scratching, meatheaded LOSER!" Gina turned around to go back to the store.

Joyce reached out and grabbed the back of Gina's shirt. "Come on, Gina. What are you going to do? Beat him up?"

"No," she said. "But I can call him some choice names and educate him. It's '*Asian* bitch,' dumb ass."

"Yeah, and then what?"

"And then he'll be enlightened and I'll feel better."

Joyce shook her head. "Forget it. You can't educate a Neanderthal. And it's the last day of school, remember?"

"I hate this school," Gina said.

Joyce snorted and smiled. Gina smiled back.

"Come on, you slow-ass Asian bitch. I'll walk you to your locker," Gina said.

"Thanks, bitch," Joyce said, and they began their slow-motion walk to their lockers.

Joyce stared at herself in the mirror hanging inside her locker. She kept brushing forward more hair to make sure the egg was covered. She didn't want a repeat performance from it. Joyce turned to Gina.

"Do I look okay?"

Gina sat on the cement floor signing Joyce's yearbook. "You look great," she said without looking up.

Joyce checked herself one last time. This was it. Fifth period. Her last chance to really see the color of John Ford Kang's eyes.

"Wish me luck," Joyce said, taking a breath.

"Luck," Gina said, still not looking up from the book.

Joyce scowled. "What are you doing? Stop writing in that. You better not be saying anything incriminating."

Gina finished with a flourish of her signature. "Come on. You can't give the guy an empty yearbook. He'll think you saved the entire thing for him."

Joyce felt anxiety creeping up on her again. "Oh, no, he's going to think I don't have any friends." She grabbed the yearbook and opened it up to blank page after blank page. "Where did you sign?" Joyce asked in a panic.

Gina stood up laughing. "Joyce, it's okay. Look, here's my entry. And I made it really big." Gina flipped to the back and showed her the page with the photograph of the orange tree that symbolized the school. "Just have him sign on that page."

Joyce scanned the entry that started with the block letters HEY, ASIAN BITCH. Joyce looked up. "Gina!"

Gina was already down the hall, waving. The bell for fifth period sounded through the open-air hallways. Gina cupped her hands near her mouth and yelled, "You can do it!"

Joyce shut the yearbook. This was it.

THREE

they had chemistry together. For this one whole school year, Joyce had been able to study John Ford Kang like the true specimen that he was. She knew every muscle twitch, every cadence of his laugh, every shirt that he owned. The only thing she hadn't been able to do was muster up the nerve to stare him in the eyes. Just the idea of it made her want to bolt from the room screaming. Joyce could hardly focus on the instructions that Mr. Blevins was giving them about how to properly store the beakers and pipettes. Luckily, Lynn, her lab partner, was good about stuff like that. She glanced at Lynn, who was squinting in concentration.

There were a few dozen Asian students at the school, a half dozen in her year, and she had shared a class with almost all of them, but she had never been partnered with one of them before. Lynn Song was the embodiment of the stereotypical Asian student. She wore thick glasses that made her already slim eyes look even narrower. Her stringy straight hair was cut into a harsh line straight across her back and hung in her face most of the time. Her radar for fashion was completely turned off, not to mention that she sported old-fashioned metal braces instead of the clear ceramic ones that weren't nearly as offensive. Lynn was nice, but even Joyce found herself trying not to laugh sometimes when Lynn was being especially earnest about a question.

Lynn and Joyce cleaned up their set of beakers, working like the good team that they were. Joyce dried while Lynn scrubbed.

"Do you have any plans for summer?" Joyce asked Lynn, trying to keep her mind off her bigger task. Joyce had planned to ask John to sign her yearbook at the end of class.

"I'm taking this accelerated summer science program at Cal Tech," Lynn said, pushing her glasses up and focusing on the beaker in her hands. Lynn's hair kept falling into her face, making her look slightly deranged. Joyce wanted to hand her a rubber band to tie back the mess.

"That sounds fun," Joyce said, watching John cross the room to his desk.

"Are you crazy?" Lynn glanced up from her task. "I think it's going to be hell, but my guidance counselor thought it would make my apps for college stronger."

Joyce dropped the paper towel to conceal her embarrassment and bent down to retrieve it.

"I just mean it'll be fun to meet other people who aren't from this school," Joyce said, standing up.

"Yeah, that's for sure," Lynn said, her eyes following two guys throwing paper balls at each other. "Hopefully there won't be as many losers."

Joyce smiled. She had to give it to Lynn. No matter how bad she might look, Lynn honestly didn't care what other people thought. She was bent on a specific Ivy League school, and everything she did was to achieve her goal. Her quiet confidence made Joyce wish she could ask for Lynn's secret formula.

They finished up silently and placed the clean beakers back into the cabinet. Joyce turned around and surveyed the room for John. He was sitting on top of his desk talking to one of his friends. He always had someone who wanted to talk to him. Even though he was Asian, he looked and acted like everyone else. Like someone who belonged in this school, in this neighborhood, with all these students. Not an immigrant that moved into the area or faked an address to attend one of the best schools in Orangedale. Maybe it was because he was only half Asian and looked like some movie star. Or maybe it was because he knew he had an exotic model mother who probably didn't cook kimchee ji-geh at home, stinking up the entire house. Joyce wandered back to her desk to retrieve her yearbook. And if John's mom didn't cook Korean food, then John's dad had to get his Korean food fix somehow because Koreans can't live without their food. The addictive combination of garlic, chili and salt must be imprinted on Koreans from birth. Maybe John's father came to their restaurant to get his Korean food fix. Would Joyce be able to spot John Ford Kang's father if she saw him?

Joyce glanced up at the clock. It was time. She pulled more of her hair forward over the zit and took a deep breath. As she walked to his desk, she held the yearbook in front of her like a shield.

She didn't want to interrupt, so she waited for him to notice. For his friend to stop explaining how to get to this amazing surfing spot down the coast. The bell was going to ring any minute. She cleared her throat. An ear-piercing, sharp alarm sounded.

John jumped off the desk and smacked right into Joyce, sending her reeling backwards and then falling to the floor.

"Oh, man. I'm sorry. I didn't even see you there." John reached out to her, offering his hand.

Without thinking, Joyce automatically reached up and grabbed the offered hand. He pulled her up in one graceful arch with a gentle and surprising strength. Joyce stood in front of him. He smiled down at her. She stared up into his eyes. Oh, Joyce thought. Oh, his eyes are amazing. Brown and green and amazing.

"You okay?" he asked.

She nodded.

"Here." He bent down and grabbed her yearbook off the floor. "Sorry about that," he said and handed her the yearbook. "That bell just makes me jump sometimes."

Joyce nodded again.

"Have a good summer," John said. He paused for a second right before he turned away. And winked.

Joyce gasped. On anyone else, the wink would have been cheesy as all hell. On anyone else, the wink would have been slimy and completely gross. On John Ford Kang, the wink was heartbreaking.

John started to walk away.

Joyce spun around and called out, "Wait!"

John paused.

Joyce raced up to him and thrust the yearbook out in front of her. "Can you sign this?"

He shrugged. "Yeah, sure. Okay." He reached for the yearbook.

Joyce immediately pulled it back and fumbled around for the spot where Gina had signed. She felt her face flaming up. "Let me find a page," she muttered.

John dropped his backpack to the floor and stood patiently. Joyce found the page with the orange tree and handed it to him. He stared down at Gina's loopy handwriting.

"Do you have a pen?" he asked.

"Oh. No." Joyce scanned the desktops and floors. There had to be one somewhere. "You wait. I go find one." Joyce wanted to bite her tongue off. Why couldn't she speak properly? What if he thought she was some FOB, fresh off the boat from Korea?

John reached down to his backpack. "No worries. I have one in my pack."

It felt like hours as Joyce stood there and watched John open his pack and extract a blue pen and then reach for the yearbook. It was another lifetime watching him carefully think about what to say and then quickly jot it down. Joyce stood in her place and gazed up at him. At his firm muscled shoulders as he leaned over the yearbook. At his long slender fingers grasping the pen. Joyce marveled at the way his dark lashes curled at the edges. Perfect.

John glanced up, sensing her eyes on him, and Joyce jerked her eyes down. She nervously reached up to tuck her hair behind her ears, but remembered to stop herself just before she revealed too much.

"Here," he said and closed the book before handing it back to her. "I didn't get a yearbook this year or I'd have you sign mine," he said apologetically. "I mean, fifty dollars for a yearbook seems extreme."

"Yeah, my mom made me get one," Joyce lied, her voice high and shrill.

Stupid, she berated herself. Here she was having her first real conversation with John and all she could come up with was that her mother made her? What about her jokes? Her cool line about summer? This wasn't going the way she had planned.

John shoved his pen into the front pocket of his backpack. "See you around," he said and gave her a nod before he turned to go.

"See you," she called after him.

He raised his hand in acknowledgement and stepped out to the hallway, disappearing into the crowd.

Joyce stood in the middle of the silent empty classroom, staring out the door. Had that really happened? Did she just talk to John Ford Kang? She stared down at the yearbook in her hands. It hadn't been executed with the suave sure lines that she had planned, and he wasn't going to see her clever note, but at least she had taken the first step. John knew who she was now.

Joyce had even touched his hand. She sniffed her palm, hoping his scent had rubbed off on her. There was only a lingering sour trace of her nervous sweat. She thought about the color of his eyes. His beautiful, gorgeous, brown-green eyes. A loopy grin spread across her face as the realization slowly spread through her body. She did it. She really did it! A giddiness made her want to whoop out loud, stretch her arms to the skies and dance like some crazy in the park. John Ford Kang had signed her yearbook!

She wanted to shout it from the center of the quad. John Ford Kang signed my yearbook! She bit down on the webbing of skin between her thumb and forefinger to keep from yelling. Carefully, she cracked open the yearbook. She flipped the pages until she found his writing.

Hey Lynn,
It was great getting to know you in Chem.
Sorry about almost killing you on the last day of school.
Have a rockin summer.

JFK

Joyce closed her eyes. Every pore of her skin stung with shame and embarrassment. Joyce covered her face with her hands in humiliation. Lynn. He thought I was Lynn. Lynn. Joyce peeked to check again. There was no doubt. *Hey Lynn.* She couldn't stop staring at the name. Lynn. Lynn Song. Lynn Song. The ugliest girl in school.

joyce rode her bike to her parents' Korean restaurant in downtown Orangedale. She took her time, wiping away the tears and forcing her mind to focus on anything besides the memory of Lynn's name. As Joyce passed by the Quick Change Oil garage, she waved at a few of the guys standing outside, dirty oil rags hanging from their back pockets. Some of the crew liked to eat lunch at her parents' place, putting money down on who could eat the most chili paste.

Jorge waved and called out, "Hey, Joyce, what time does Helen's shift start?"

Another guy let loose a wolf whistle at the mention of Helen's name.

As Joyce waved and pedaled away, Jorge called after

her, "Tell your sister I'm still waiting for an answer to my marriage proposal."

A block later, she passed a convenience store parking lot packed with middle school students celebrating the beginning of vacation with slushies and candy. Joyce longed for a chocolate bar, but the thought of listening to all those excited voices forced her to pass. A longing for the simpler days of middle school unleashed another set of tears.

Helen and Joyce had both been forced to start over at new schools after Joyce's family had bought the restaurant in the zip code that would allow their children to attend some of the best schools in Los Angeles County. For two whole glorious years, Joyce went to the middle school where no one knew about Helen Park. Joyce had been herself, and that had been good enough. It was only after Joyce entered high school that the comparisons started up again.

When Joyce first started at Orangedale High, she had joined the same clubs and played softball, just like Helen. With each introduction, Joyce was asked if she was really Helen's sister, as though she might be the one confused. The more Helen tried to include Joyce, the worse Joyce felt. Eventually, Joyce realized there was no point in torturing herself and dropped out of everything. If Helen had asked a boy to sign her yearbook, he would have never gotten her name confused with anyone else.

Joyce turned into a strip mall and rode down the empty alley at the back of the building. As she approached the back door to the restaurant, Joyce could hear the sound of pots clanging and loud Korean music drifting out from the screen door. Joyce hopped off her bike and ran her hands over her face to clear any trace of her crying. With a deep breath, she pushed open the screen door. The pungent odor of chili, onions and garlic immediately saturated her senses.

"Hi," she called out as she parked her bike in the storage room, next to the sacks of rice.

"Joyce," her mother called.

"Yes, Uhmma?" Joyce walked into the kitchen.

Uhmma and Mrs. Lee, Gina's mother, were sitting on large overturned white buckets, peeling onions. Their kerchiefs held back their hair, and they both wore matching red and blue aprons with the restaurant name, Arirang, across the front.

"Apa filled all the saltshakers already. Set them on the table after you eat." Uhmma stood up and set the paring knife on the counter. She walked over and stared intently into Joyce's face.

"How was school?"

Joyce shrugged, unable to meet her mother's eyes, focusing her entire being on keeping the waterworks under control.

"Something is wrong? I had a bad dream about you last night." Uhmma claimed to have special psychic abilities, a sixth sense that could tell when her daughters were in trouble. Uhmma's eyes zeroed in on Joyce's temple. "What did you do to your face?"

Joyce stepped away. "Nothing!"

Uhmma followed Joyce around the kitchen and finally caught her at the rice cooker. She pulled back Joyce's hair.

"Ai-ya, Joyce." Uhmma clucked her tongue. "Why do you always pick? Leave it alone and it will go away faster."

"No, it won't," Joyce muttered and continued to scoop rice into her bowl to fix herself some bi-bim bop. Uhmma returned to her makeshift stool and started talking to Mrs. Lee loudly. "Joyce thinks she is the only one who suffers from pimples. I tell her not to pick, but does she listen? Was I not a teenager once?"

"I used to have pimples that covered all my face and

even my back!" Mrs. Lee said. She quickly peeled the onion and dropped it into a large stainless-steel bowl. "Eugenia takes after her father with her skin. Still so clear, like when she was a baby."

Joyce spooned vegetables, some meat and a dollop of chili paste on top of her rice from a prep counter loaded with various containers of Korean banchan like marinated vegetables and appetizers.

Mrs. Lee continued, "Eugenia only got my body and round face. She is always dieting and trying to suck in her cheeks." Mrs. Lee laughed and showed Uhmma.

Joyce ignored Uhmma and Mrs. Lee making fun of their daughters. She walked out of the kitchen and stepped into the front dining room. Behind the register counter, Apa was sitting on a stool and reading a book that he had been toting around for weeks now, taking it out whenever he had a chance. Joyce had never seen him this intrigued by a book before and tried to ask him what it was about since she couldn't decipher the Korean characters. "Good mystery," was all Apa would say.

"Hi, Apa," Joyce said and stirred her chili paste into the rice.

Apa looked up from his book and smiled. "How was your last day of school?"

"Fine," she said and leaned her back against the counter. She looked around for Andy; Uhmma usually picked him up and brought him to the restaurant.

"Where's Andy?" Joyce asked.

"He is at the basketball courts at school with some friends."

"What?" Joyce straightened up. "How come I had to come to work, and Andy didn't?"

Apa shook his head and returned to his book. "Ai, Joyce, he is still a little boy. Let him enjoy some free time."

"What about my free time?"

"Tomorrow. You can be off tomorrow."

"All day?" Joyce brightened.

Apa sighed. "I need some help at dinner."

Joyce knew she shouldn't complain, but helping out at the restaurant was really starting to become a drag. Su Yon, their former waitress, had left without any notice over a month ago. Her leaving had placed a hardship on everyone, especially Helen and Joyce, as they filled in with extra shifts. But no one complained about the former helper who had become a part of the family and Helen's best friend. The restaurant felt so empty without Su Yon's joking banter and considerate gestures. Su Yon had not explained why she was leaving, only came in one day in tears telling them that she was moving away. They had all assumed it had something to do with her controlling mother. There was a small help-wanted sign in the window, but no one had answered that sign or any of the ads they had placed in the Korean news-papers.

Joyce stared into her bi-bim bop. "Can Gina come and keep me company this afternoon?"

Apa nodded. "You have to promise to do all your work."

"I will," Joyce said and picked up the phone by the register.

"Hey, come over. Sorry. I know. I'll tell you later." Joyce glanced at her father. "Just come over. Okay. Bye."

Joyce went to one of the corner booths with her bowl of bi-bim bop and sat down. She stared out through the large panel of glass at the front of the restaurant. Joyce had been unable to face Gina after school. She had skipped sixth-period gym and gone to clean out her locker early. She left a note for Gina saying that she would call later. It would have been too painful to tell Gina that she had just wasted fifty dollars on a boy who couldn't even get her name straight.

When Joyce had first revealed her crush, there had

been a lot of ribbing from Gina. [John was one of the few popular Asian Americans at Orangedale High amongst all the wealthy "new-un sahram" or snowmen, as so many of their Korean friends called them. Gina called John a banana, yellow on the outside, white on the inside, who would never get caught dead hanging out with some Asian chick. He seemed to be always dating a blonde. The lighter the hair, the better. Joyce took a bite of her rice, savoring the spicy chili paste that would make her breath foul in about two seconds. He might date blondes, but maybe, just maybe, someday, he could fall in love with another Korean. There had to be a part of him that felt comforted by being around Koreans.

"We are his people," Joyce had pointed out, and Gina burst into laughter.

Joyce took another bite of her spicy chili paste rice and wondered if John had a favorite Korean dish.

Joyce and Gina went from table to table setting out the refilled saltshakers and topping off the soy sauce containers.

"He thought you were Lynn Song?" Gina said

incredulously. She leaned forward. "Did the jerk even look at your face?"

"Yes," Joyce said. "He was actually really nice."

Gina jutted out her chin and swiveled her head like a snake about to strike. "Nice is someone who knows your name. Nice is NOT someone who confuses you with the only other freakin' Asian girl in your class. Don't even get me started on this, Joyce."

"Shhh," Joyce whispered, glancing over at the kitchen. Last thing she needed was for her parents to overhear.

"So what did you do with the yearbook?" Gina whispered, her lips barely moving.

Joyce pretended to concentrate on making sure the soy sauce didn't drip. "I, uh, threw it away," Joyce lied.

"Threw it away!" Gina yelled. "You threw away fifty bucks!"

Joyce put down the soy sauce. "Stop it, Gina. Just drop it, okay?"

Gina bit down on the insides of her cheeks, her lips puckered in annoyance.

Joyce moved to the next table with the tray of salt-shakers. Gina stayed in her spot. Wasting money was always a sore subject for Gina. Ever since her father had taken off five years ago, money was always on Gina's mind. Gina only worked part-time on weekends because she wanted to focus on getting the grades to go to college. Like everything Gina tackled, she expected nothing but the best. Gina was not going to settle for any state school. She was aiming for a school on the East Coast, a private school with a huge endowment for financial aid.

"I'll pay you back," Joyce said, unable to meet Gina's eyes.

Gina walked over to her. "It's not about the money."

"Then why are you all bent out of shape? It's my money. I can spend it the way that I want."

Gina leaned forward. "But you spent it on some idiot that doesn't even know your name."

"So?" Joyce said. "I got to see his eyes. And they are amazing. They're brown and green—"

"Whose eyes?" Andy asked, popping into the conversation.

Joyce and Gina jumped back, knocking over some of the saltshakers.

Joyce frowned. "Jeez, Andy. Don't sneak up on us like that."

"I wasn't sneaking," Andy said and shoved an entire steamed dumpling into his mouth.

"Why do you have to eat that mandu like a Neanderthal?" Joyce asked.

Andy opened his mouth to show her the contents.

"Joyce, you have to throw salt over your shoulder," Gina interrupted. "Which shoulder is it?"

"Scram, Andy."

"Uhmma said that I should help you."

Gina tossed salt over both shoulders.

"I don't need help. Why don't you go pretend to play basketball? That's all you and your midget friends can do, anyway."

Andy threw up his middle finger.

Joyce grabbed it.

Andy wrestled it away and walked off. "Must be your time of the month!"

"Shut up, shrimp!" Joyce said and pretended to lunge after him.

Andy dashed into the kitchen.

Gina handed Joyce some salt. "Come on. Toss it or else you'll have bad luck all summer."

"Like it's not following me around, right now?" Joyce said and tossed some salt over both shoulders.

Gina looked over at the kitchen, double-checking for Andy. "Is he really starting middle school next year?"

Joyce moved to another table with the tray and set down a saltshaker. "Yeah."

Gina laughed. "And he still wants to be a professional basketball player?"

Joyce nodded.

"What is with your family?" Gina asked.

"What do you mean?"

"Deep denial," Gina said, shaking her head.

"What are you talking about?" Joyce asked.

Gina put one hand on her hip. "You eat chocolate all the time and complain about zits. You spend fifty bucks on some half Korean guy who will not even look in the direction of another Asian, and your brother wants to be a professional basketball player even though he's as tall as the table," Gina said.

"Oh, please," Joyce said and pretended to gag. "Like you're some pillar of wisdom? Remember the time you spent all that money on some designer bra that was supposed to give you cleavage and all you got was a backache from the straps being so tight?"

Gina shuddered. "Okay, okay, I don't want to relive that purchase. I'm still reeling from all the money I threw away." Gina held up her hand. "Let's change the subject. I still can't believe John Ford Kang thought you were Lynn. Doesn't she wear glasses?"

Joyce nodded. "And she has really bad teeth. Have you ever seen them? They're so crooked, and she has these bucks in the front that practically scream rabbit. I don't know why she didn't get the clear braces."

"Maybe she couldn't afford them," Gina said quietly, fiddling with a saltshaker.

Joyce quickly changed the subject, aware that she had stumbled onto another sensitive topic. "Her glasses are so thick they're bulletproof. Look at me. Do I look anything like Lynn Song?"

Gina smiled, her lips carefully sealed shut against her misaligned teeth. "Maybe you could use some glamming up."

Joyce frowned. "Glamming up? What is that? A verb? Are you trying to tell me something?"

"No, but maybe you could try and look a little more"—Gina waved her hands in the air, trying to find the right word—"put together."

"Put together?" Joyce could feel the anger tightening in her throat, even though she knew Gina was right. "Are you trying to tell me I look like a loser? That I don't have an alibi? That I'm U. G. L. Y.?"

"No! I just mean we could use this summer to kind

of transform ourselves. You know, like a makeover or something. And definitely a new wardrobe. You have this amazing bod, and you always hide it in baggy jeans and T-shirts. Don't you want our senior year to rock?"

"Yeah, but it's not like we're going to get popular overnight just because we dress differently or style our hair a certain way. I stopped believing in that summer Cinderella dream in middle school," Joyce lied, purposefully keeping her voice gruff and low. She knew if Gina even got a whiff of her plans to get rid of her chubby knees over the summer in an attempt at transforming herself for senior year, it would become a full-blown episode of *Makeover Madness*. Gina would have an exercise plan worked out, with daily eating charts, and would make Joyce shop all the time to buy the best clothes at the cheapest prices. Gina always went the whole nine yards and then some.

Gina chuckled to herself. "Remember that summer before eighth grade when we got those bad perms?"

"Trying to get that corkscrew hair effect." Joyce laughed. "God, that was awful. And then you made us get another perm to try and correct the first bad one."

"Hey, that wasn't just my idea. Wait," Gina said,

her neck craning to look out the window. "Speaking of makeovers, I think your aunt just pulled up."

Joyce whirled around. "Gomo? What is she doing here so early?"

An older woman in a matching argyle sweater suit was just stepping out of her Mercedes.

"Maybe she wants to put her order in before the dinner rush," Gina said.

"I better warn Uhmma and Apa." Joyce rushed off to the kitchen and poked her head in. "Gomo is here!"

Uhmma looked up from the stove. "What?"

Apa was sitting at the back table eating and reading his book.

"She just pulled up in front," Joyce said.

Apa quickly stashed his book under some napkins and stood up.

"What is she doing here so early?" Uhmma pulled off her kerchief in a panic and began madly fluffing up her hair with her fingertips.

Joyce turned around to go back to the front but spotted Andy crouched behind the register counter. "Andy!" Joyce yelled. "You little spy!"

Andy whispered, "Michael's here!"

Joyce smiled despite herself. Andy and Joyce called

their aunt by a code name for the singer who had altered his appearance beyond recognition.

Joyce crooked her finger at him and Andy stood up reluctantly. As weird as Gomo was, she was still their aunt who had made it possible for the entire family to immigrate to the United States, and Gomo wasn't about to let anyone forget.

F I V E

on-young!" Gomo called out as she pushed open the glass front door of the restaurant.

Joyce stepped forward to greet her aunt and bowed deeply from the waist as she said, "On-young-ha-say-yo, Gomo."

Gina waved from the table where she was topping off one of the soy sauce containers. "Hi, Gomo," Gina said.

Gomo frowned at Gina's casual greeting.

"Joyce-ya, go get your uhmma and apa," Gomo commanded and walked over to a table, carefully brushing off a chair cushion before sitting down. Gomo never entered the kitchen, preferring to be treated like a customer. A customer who ate at their restaurant nearly every day and never paid, but a customer all the same. Gomo's heavily made-up face hardly moved when she spoke. "I have exciting news for everyone!"

Joyce turned around to rush her parents, but they were already stepping out of the kitchen with Mrs. Lee close behind. Uhmma bowed deeply from the waist, her hair brushed back, a coat of lipstick shining and her apron off.

"On-young-ha-say-yo, Gomo," Uhmma said.

"Oh-young-ha-say-yo," Mrs. Lee chimed.

Uhmma rushed over to the table where Gomo was sitting. "Is everything all right? You are here so early today."

Gomo examined Uhmma closely. "You look tired, Helen's uhmma. Have you been applying the cream I gave you?"

Uhmma smiled awkwardly and nodded.

Apa walked over to his older sister and patted her hand to distract her gaze. "Gomo, what would you like to eat tonight? We have mackerel, fresh. It came in today. Shall I grill it up for you?"

Gomo shook her head and motioned for Apa to sit down. She carefully ran her fingers across her brow, sweeping aside any stray hairs. She leaned forward. "I have exciting news!"

Everyone leaned toward her, waiting.

Gomo scanned her audience. "Where is Helen?"

"She is at school today," Uhmma explained.

Gomo's shoulders dropped a bit in disappointment. Helen had always been Gomo's favorite, and she did not go out of her way to hide that fact.

"I will make sure to call her," Gomo said to herself and carefully smoothed back her hair once more.

Andy couldn't take it. "What news?" he yelled and pushed forward.

Gomo snapped her head toward him. Uhmma pushed Andy behind her chair.

"I," Gomo said slowly. "I have"—she paused, making sure all eyes were on her—"I have won the lottery."

Screams erupted from everyone. Andy and Joyce jumped up and down. Uhmma and Apa leaped out of their chairs. Mrs. Lee clapped her hands and began crying. Joyce ran to Gina and hugged her. They pulled back and started shrieking in unison and jumping around the dining room, their arms flailing high in the air.

"Shhhh," Uhmma said. "Shhh. Please, quiet down so we can hear."

Joyce and Gina breathlessly walked over to the table where Gomo was sitting.

Gomo was smoothing out the lottery ticket on the table, her shoulders hunched forward, her forearms protectively blocking anyone from getting too close.

"I must take this ticket to the claim office, but I had to first stop to tell my family the wonderful news," Gomo said, her face barely budging into a smile.

Andy elbowed Joyce in the side and gave her the robot Gomo smile that could hardly be called a smile unless you knew that Gomo's face wouldn't budge more than an inch from all the Botox she got injected to make herself look younger.

Gomo pointed at the ticket. "I only miss this number, but everything else is a perfect match."

"WHAT?" Andy pushed forward. "You mean you didn't get all the numbers?" He stared down intently at the ticket.

Gina started laughing.

Andy frowned at Gomo. "But you just said you won the lottery!"

Gomo pulled the ticket off the table and slipped it into her purse. "The man at the 7-Eleven said I won a great deal of money."

Andy snarled in disgust. "It's not millions! You didn't win. You said—"

Uhmma grabbed Andy by the shoulders and pushed

him in the direction of the kitchen. "Go and get Gomo some water." She turned her attention back to Gomo. "This is the most exciting news, Gomo! Do you want Apa to go with you to the lottery office?"

Gomo shook her head. "I can handle it myself. I thought my family would be happy for me."

"We are happy for you, Gomo!" Uhmma said quickly. "That Andy is always trying to be funny. He is becoming a teenager. You know how that is, Gomo."

Gomo's eyebrows moved a fraction of an inch. Gina snorted so loud Joyce had to elbow her.

Gomo stood up and the crowd stepped back to give her room.

"I was hoping everyone would be very pleased. It is important to share good fortune with family. We must give thanks and honor those who are most precious to us," Gomo lectured, her eyes scanning the room. Joyce quickly pasted on a wide smile when Gomo's gaze turned in her direction. "Next Monday, we will have a special celebration dinner. I have plans to give you all very special gifts." Gomo lifted her finger and wagged it for emphasis. "Very special gifts."

Everyone stood outside the restaurant waving as Gomo pulled her Mercedes out of the parking spot and drove out to the street. When her taillight could barely be seen, Uhmma finally dropped her hand. Everyone headed back into the restaurant.

"That was a nice distraction," Uhmma said.

Andy grumbled loudly. "She said she won the lottery. What a lie."

Apa bonked Andy in the head with his knuckle.

"Ai-ya!" Andy said, reaching up to the sore spot.

Gina and Joyce went back to setting the saltshakers on the tables.

"She probably won, like, ten thousand dollars or something," Gina said.

"Yeah," Joyce said and began unscrewing the top to the soy sauce container. "It's funny how even that much money sounds like nothing after you think you're getting millions."

Gina raised one eyebrow. "Did you think you were going to get millions?"

Joyce felt a flush creeping up her neck as she recalled her first thoughts at the news of the lottery. She carefully poured the soy sauce. "Well, not me. But I did think that Gomo was going to give my family some money." Joyce looked up at Gina. "I mean, can you imagine if Gomo really had won the lottery? She would be filthy rich. Don't you think she would share some of that with us?"

Gina wrinkled her nose. "I suppose. But you know how wealthy people are. The more they have, the more they think they don't have enough." Gina did her best Orangedale long blond hair flip. "Ohmygod, like I can't believe they are so charging fifty dollars for a yearbook. But look at me in my designer everything and this handbag that, like, cost three thousand dollars."

Joyce laughed uncomfortably. She didn't tell Gina that John had refused to pay for the yearbook this year.

"I wonder what Gomo is going to get us? Very special presents?" Joyce wondered.

Gina put down a saltshaker and set her face into a frozen mask. Barely moving her lips, she said, "Maybe she'll take you for a makeover."

Joyce laughed for real this time. "God, I think her face has gotten worse."

"How many surgeries has she had?" Gina asked.

"Eight," Andy chimed in, popping out from behind the cash register. "Well, eight, if you don't count the time she had to fix her messed-up nose job."

Joyce cracked up. "Remember that? She sounded like Darth Vader until they fixed the airway."

Andy walked out from behind the counter doing

the Darth Vader breathing. "Ewhhh-I-ehhh-going to-ewhhhhhh-sue-ehhhh-that bad-eh-gag-eh-doctor."

Gina shook her head. "Do you even remember what Gomo looked like before all the plastic surgery?"

"I think we have pictures somewhere from before she came to America," Joyce said.

Andy jumped into the air, arm stretched out, hand quickly flipping down in a pretend shot at the basket. "She looked just like Joyce," Andy said.

Joyce whirled around. "She did not!"

Andy grinned. "That's what Uhmma and Apa say."

"Shut up!" Joyce yelled.

Andy swaggered toward the kitchen. "Hey, if Michael can try and make herself beautiful, then you can try and make yourself beautiful, Joyce."

Andy ducked into the kitchen just as Joyce hurled a saltshaker in his direction.

[the dinner rush was just beginning when Helen hurried through the back door into the kitchen, her bright tropical-colored book bags hanging off her arms. Joyce stood waiting on an order of bulgoki to take to table five and watched her sister struggle with the gaudy bags that she had received as a gift from Gomo a month ago. Leave it to Helen, the respectful older sister, to actually use the bags instead of hiding them in the back of their closet like Joyce did with most of the things that Gomo had bestowed upon her.

"Sorry I'm late," Helen said breathlessly. She threw her bags into the storage room and grabbed a red and blue apron off the hook.

Even when Helen was rushed and wearing awful

colors, she still managed to look like she had just stepped out of an Asian cosmetics ad. Her complexion was flawless, with a natural faint blush of pink on her cheeks. Her large light brown eyes and dark black hair accented her heart-shaped face. Sometimes, when Helen was concentrating on something, Joyce would find herself staring at Helen and secretly cursing the universe for its unfairness. While Helen and Joyce certainly looked alike, everything about Helen was better. Helen was the deluxe to Joyce's standard model. The upgraded version. Helen's features were more symmetrical—her eyes larger, the rose-petal pout of her lips fuller, her skin clearer. Their bodies were similarly lean and strong, except that Helen had received the slightly larger breasts, the longer legs and the knees without the fat. Joyce would have settled for the larger brain, but even that small consolation had been robbed from her.

Uhmma plated the barbecued beef and added the sprigs of parsley and green scallions to the side of the platter. Just as she was about to hand it off to Joyce, Helen stepped in and grabbed it.

"Here, let me help you, Joyce. I can take this out. What table is it?"

Joyce grabbed the platter back from Helen. "It's my order, Helen. Back off."

Helen frowned. "I was just trying to give you a break since I'm so late."

Uhmma stepped in between them. "Joyce, you take that out. Helen, sit down and eat before you start working. Did you have lunch? What kind of summer research group keeps you out until dinnertime?" Uhmma ushered Helen over to the corner table, carrying a bowl of soup.

"It's okay, Uhmma. Dr. Josen said this meeting went especially late because she wanted to train us. We're not going to have these long hours all summer," Helen said, sitting down.

Uhmma sat down next to her. "Dr. Josen already accepted you? I thought she was only interviewing people."

"She is, but she knew she wanted me, so I just had to fill out the paperwork."

"They are going to pay you for all your hard work?" Uhmma asked.

Helen sighed. "No, Uhmma. This is an internship. She only picks ten students out of the entire college to help her with the research project. I should be paying her for letting me work with her. I'm the only sophomore on the project. The rest are seniors or graduates."

Joyce walked slowly toward the door to the dining

room. Summer research group? Joyce groaned inwardly. There goes driving to the beach.

"You are working too hard. Maybe you should rest this summer," Uhmma said, worried.

"It keeps my mind busy," Helen said.

"Did you hear from Su Yon?" Uhmma asked quietly.

There was no answer from Helen.

"Gomo came to the store today with some exciting news!" Uhmma said, changing the subject.

Joyce quickened her steps and walked out into the dining room.

The dinner rush was particularly busy that night. The end of the school year meant celebrations. Large groups of families with kids in their graduation best flanked by grandmothers and grandfathers crowded the restaurant, blocking the entrance. Helen and Joyce rushed around seating people and then taking orders. Apa worked the register and carried orders out to the tables when Helen and Joyce got too busy. Mrs. Lee plated the small dishes of banchan to be served before the meal and prepped the vegetables, while Uhmma managed the grill and stove. Andy stood next to Juan Carlos, their evening dishwashing helper, and loaded up the trays with dirty dishes.

Mrs. Kim, a regular customer, was with her niece and nephew and their family.

"Joyce-ya," Mrs. Kim called and waved Joyce over. Joyce nodded to her and finished taking an order from a young college couple. She walked over to Mrs. Kim.

"On-young-ha-say-yo, Mrs. Kim," Joyce said. "Would you like me to take your orders now?"

Mrs. Kim grinned and waved her empty shoju glass. "Go and get that beautiful sister of yours," Mrs. Kim slurred and turned to her niece and nephew. "This girl." Mrs. Kim looked up at Joyce. "Not her, but her sister. This girl, Helen, could be the next Miss Korea. She is so smart and beautiful and cha-keh. You meet her and see what a good example she is for you two."

Joyce walked back to the kitchen. Helen was helping Mrs. Lee finish another set of banchan to be loaded onto the tray.

"Mrs. Kim wants you," Joyce reported.

Helen looked up. "Isn't she at your table?"

"So? She said she wants you."

Helen sighed and finished loading the tray with the small dishes. "I'll go say hello. Will you take this to table ten?"

Joyce took the tray from Helen. "Fine."

By the end of the long night, everyone was exhausted.

Apa locked the front door and then went back to the kitchen to help Uhmma and Mrs. Lee clean up. Helen vacuumed the dining room floor while Joyce wiped down the tables. Andy was fast asleep on one of the booth benches.

Helen unplugged the vacuum cord and started rolling it up. She looked over at Joyce. "Are you going to stay mad at me all night?"

Joyce stopped wiping down the table and asked, "How come you just left me this morning?"

Helen sighed. "Joyce, I called for you three times and then waited and waited."

"I was in the bathroom."

"For over an hour!"

Joyce finished with her table and moved farther away from Helen to the next table.

Helen walked over. "Look, I'm sorry, but I had to go or else Andy would have been late for school and I would have been late for my interview. I tried to tell you."

Joyce whirled away from her angrily. "You did not try to tell me! You left me! I forgot my yearbook and backpack today because I had to rush out of the apartment after you ditched me."

Helen leaned her weight back on one foot and

crossed her arms. "Look, Joyce, you have to stop projecting your anger onto me. Take responsibility for your mistakes."

Joyce waved her finger in Helen's face. "Don't even try your psychobabble on me, Helen."

"Stop being so childish," Helen said. "I swear you regress every time I talk to you."

"You want to play that game?"

"What game?"

Joyce crossed her arms in front of her chest. "Fine. Guess what! I need the car this summer."

"Stop it, Joyce. You know I have this summer internship."

"Yeah, well, I have a lot of meetings this summer, too!" Joyce screeched.

Helen pressed her lips together and gazed up at the ceiling. "Okay, Joyce." Helen lowered her eyes, her face softened in sympathy. "Maybe we can coordinate our schedules."

Joyce focused on refolding her wet rag. She didn't know what felt worse, Helen's pity or the thought of losing out on the car all summer. Why did Joyce always end up in this position? Just once, Joyce wanted to feel like what she had to do was just as important as Helen's schedule. That she mattered just as much as Helen.

"I could drop you off at school or wherever you need to go. Or you could drop me, but then you would have to double back," Helen said, already trying to work out the logistics.

"Forget it," Joyce said and walked away.

Uhmma and Apa had Helen drive Joyce and Andy home while they finished closing the restaurant. All the way back to the apartment, Joyce refused to say a word to Helen.

Helen pulled into their parking space in front of the apartment building. She turned in her seat and faced Joyce.

"Look, Joyce, I'm really sorry. I've been feeling pretty crappy lately. I know you think I always get my way, but it's not like that. I need to do this internship for a lot of reasons. I'm trying to work something out."

Joyce crossed her arms in front of her chest and turned away.

"Can we just talk for a minute?"

Joyce held up her hand, fingers spread wide, inches from Helen's face.

Helen clenched her jaw and turned away, opening the car door to step out. Joyce reached back and gently shook Andy awake. The three walked into their apartment complex, heading for the outside set of stairs that led up to their second-floor apartment. In the building to the right of theirs, just beyond the cement courtyard that used to be a pool before the landlord filled it in, a soft red light shined out of a small window.

Helen glanced over as she started up the steps and commented, "Who has a red light in their room? That's strange."

Joyce glanced over at the light. Sam must be working late on his photographs. Everyone in the entire apartment complex knew Sam developed his pictures in a makeshift darkroom that was his bathroom. He was going into his senior year of high school like Joyce, but he didn't attend Orangedale. He didn't need to go to a school like Orangedale when his photographs were going to get him into art school. At least, that was what everyone thought, everyone who knew him, except for Helen. She was always so busy and focused on her own work, she never had the time to find out what other people were doing.

Joyce started up the stairs behind Helen and Andy. Everyone seemed to have goals. Dreams. Talent. Helen had taken one psychology class and already she was part of a research group after one year. Gina always put a hundred percent effort into whatever she set her mind to, like going to an East Coast college that she had already picked out, and attended every informational meeting. Even Andy knew he wanted to be a professional basketball player and practiced as much as he could. Joyce had no idea what she wanted. She couldn't even choose an outfit other than jeans and a T-shirt every morning. What were her dreams and goals? Except talking to John Ford Kang, which had been a disaster, Joyce could only think about driving the car this summer, and even that was going to be taken away. And once again, Helen's plans mattered more.

andy, stop playing that video game and get dressed," Uhmma called out. Joyce poked her head out of the bedroom that she shared with Helen to find Uhmma running from the bathroom down the hallway in her slip. Even from the back, Joyce could tell that Uhmma had hair-sprayed into place the helmet hair she wore for public appearances. Monday was the one day of the week when the restaurant was closed. And in the summers, when there was no school, Mondays felt better than a weekend.

Apa stepped out of their bedroom in a new blue suit and new black wing-tip shoes.

"Apa, tell Andy to get ready," Uhmma said as she skirted around him and entered their bedroom.

Apa nodded and walked toward Andy's room. Joyce stepped out into the hall and evaluated the new clothes that Gomo had dropped off for Apa earlier in the day.

"Looking good, Apa," Joyce said.

Apa grinned and lifted the lapels of his suit. "Gomo picked out a nice one this time."

Joyce smiled. You never knew what Gomo would find. Most of the time she would hit a sale and come bearing clothes in either atrocious colors or the wrong sizes. As Apa walked past her to Andy's room, Joyce felt there was something else different about him besides the clothes, but she couldn't quite place her finger on it.

Uhmma stepped out into the hallway in a maroon dress and black pumps.

"Joyce," she said, rushing over, "where is your sister?"

"She went to wait outside." Joyce smoothed her black, knee-length skirt and wondered if Uhmma would notice that she was wearing the outfit they had picked out together last month.

"Go wait with her," Uhmma said and ran into Andy's room. "Aigoo! Both of you stop staring at that video game. Andy, get dressed."

"Shoot that one, Andy," Joyce could hear Apa say. "He is almost at the next level."

Joyce turned and walked out into the living room. She went to the large window next to the front door and looked out. Helen was sitting on the concrete steps staring at the sky, her hands clasped together. Helen had been doing a lot of that lately. Escaping out to the stairs when she needed to be alone. Joyce wondered why Helen even bothered to live at home. It would have been a lot easier on both of them if Helen just moved to the dorms, but then again, it would have cost more money.

Joyce watched as Helen pressed her fingers to the corner of her eyes as if she might be crying.

Without thinking, Joyce tapped on the window, and Helen turned around.

Joyce pressed her nose and lips to the window and ballooned out her cheeks into the squirrelly face that they both knew so well. The same face Helen had made so many times to make Joyce stop crying or to make her laugh when Helen took care of her and Andy while their parents worked long hours.

Helen shook her head and grinned.

"We are late. Hurry," Uhmma said, rushing up behind Joyce. Apa and Andy followed close behind. Andy's eyes were still glued to his handheld video game. They all gathered at the front door.

"Ready?" Apa said and reached for the doorknob.

Uhmma grabbed the video game out of Andy's hands and threw it on the couch. Andy stared at his empty hands, his thumbs pressing air.

Uhmma slung her purse over her shoulder. "Now we are ready," she said.

As they drove closer to the Koreatown neighborhood in Los Angeles, the signs slowly changed from English to Hangul symbols until it was hard to tell that they were still in America. All around them, the signs, the people, the building hearkened to another culture.

Helen pointed at a beauty shop. "Hey, Joyce, remember when we got our ears pierced at that place?"

Joyce smiled. "Yeah, and you made me go first because you were too chicken."

"You were always braver than me," Helen said.

"I think that experience made me swear off inflicting pain on myself for the rest of my life." Joyce grimaced. "Uhmma and Apa will never have to worry about me getting a tattoo, that's for sure."

Helen chuckled. "See? I did do you a favor."

Apa turned into a large outdoor mall complex. They could see Gomo clutching two large shopping bags standing outside a large ornate façade that perfectly replicated a traditional Korean building, from the sweeping roofline to the large double wooden doors.

Uhmma quickly flipped down the visor to check her makeup in the mirror. "I hope Gomo has not been waiting long."

Apa turned into a parking spot. "Yuh-boh, do not worry. We are celebrating tonight."

"Why do we always have to celebrate at a Korean restaurant?" Andy complained, pulling at the collar of his white dress shirt. "We only eat Korean food EVERY DAY!"

Uhmma turned in her seat to give him a dark scowl. "Andy! I do not want to hear you talking like that in front of Gomo."

Andy let his head loll forward. "Okay, okay."

They stepped out of the car and walked toward Gomo, who waved frantically at them, as though they might miss her.

"How much you want to bet Michael has some ugly sale clothes for us in those shopping bags?" Andy whispered to Joyce.

"No way," Joyce whispered back. "Did you see what Apa is wearing? She's flush with lottery money."

"Gomo!" Uhmma called and ran forward. "Have you been waiting long?"

Andy spoke out of the side of his mouth. "Michael can't help herself."

"Okay, you two, stop," Helen said.

"Yes, Mom." Joyce grinned.

Joyce and Andy took their turn bowing and hugging Gomo, who stood stock still and firmly patted their backs like she was slapping dust from a rug. When it was Helen's turn, Gomo reached out and cupped Helen's face in her hands, giving Helen a kiss on the cheek.

"You are feeling better?" Gomo asked.

Helen nodded as she forced a smile to her face.

Apa cleared his throat loudly and pulled open one of the large wooden doors to the restaurant.

Gomo ignored him and continued to hold Helen's face. "Good," Gomo said firmly. "You will have many, many friends in your lifetime. Do not trouble yourself with just one."

"Yes, Gomo," Helen said.

Apa began coughing and wheezing, grabbing at the collar of his new white dress shirt. Uhmma touched his elbow to calm him down.

"Let us go inside," Gomo said and led the way into the darkened dining room.

Once they were seated and their dinner orders placed, they sat with their teacups in front of them.

Gomo clinked the side of her water glass with her chopsticks.

"I would like to make an announcement," she said. Gomo looked at each one of them, her face so heavily made up it resembled the Korean masks that were hanging on the walls as decoration. Joyce couldn't understand how someone who cared so much about the way she looked couldn't get some decent makeup lessons.

"I am getting older," Gomo said. "You are my only family."

Everyone nodded. Gomo was a widow and had never been able to have children of her own.

"And with Uncle Joe watching over us, I feel I do not have many more years left."

Uhmma complained loudly, "No, no, do not say those things, Gomo. You are still so strong and healthy."

Andy kicked Joyce under the table. Uncle Joe was Gomo's third American husband and third Joe. Although no one was certain if all of Gomo's husbands were really named Joe or if Gomo just insisted on calling them all Joe. Gomo had lived with the third Uncle Joe in San Francisco, and he had been more a myth than reality. They had only met him a few times before he passed away and Gomo moved down to L.A. Andy used to joke that Uncle Joe was really a life-size blowup G.I. Joe doll because whenever they did see him for the holidays, he was always dressed in his army fatigues and watching football.

Gomo held up her hand to silence Uhmma. "I am getting older, but there are still some things that I would like to do before my time comes to join Uncle Joe. I want to make sure each one of you gets their wish," Gomo said. "I would like to make your lives better."

Make our lives better? Joyce glanced up from playing with her napkin as she daydreamed about John Ford Kang surfing. Apa and Uhmma glanced at each other. Helen was staring off into the restaurant, while Andy nervously jiggled one leg.

Joyce held her breath. Maybe she was going to give them a million dollars!

Gomo reached down and pulled up one shopping bag. "Apa already received his gifts, but I want to give Andy and Helen their gifts tonight."

Andy sat up straighter in his seat.

Gomo handed the bag to Uhmma and gestured that she should pass it on to Helen.

Uhmma handed Helen the bag.

"Gam-sa-ham-nee-da, Gomo," Helen said and bowed her head before accepting the bag. Helen reached in and pulled out a large gift-wrapped box. Andy nudged

Joyce in the side. Helen unwrapped the box and carefully lifted the lid. Inside was a beautifully embroidered white silk traditional Korean dress.

Uhmma gasped and brought her hands to her lips. "Gomo, you should not have spent this much on Helen's hanbok!"

Helen stood up and held the traditional Korean outfit in front of her. The hanbok was truly stunning, with tiny embroidered blush pink flowers circling the entire hem and sleeves of the dress. Joyce couldn't help herself and reached out to touch the fabric. The thick, rich silk shone with a soft gleam, the cool smoothness light as rain on Joyce's fingertips.

Helen remained standing with the dress so that Uhmma and Apa could admire it, but Joyce could tell there was something wrong. The set of Helen's lips, slightly off center, and the way her eyes were painfully open and alert. Joyce couldn't believe that Helen wouldn't like a hanbok that gorgeous.

Gomo waved her hand at the box. "Pull out the book!"

Uhmma reached over and pulled out a black binder. Helen carefully folded up the dress and set it back into the box. She took the binder from Uhmma and sat down.

"I have taken care of the fees. You only need to contact Mrs. Hahn and she will arrange all of the meetings," Gomo said.

Helen carefully opened the book and turned to page after page of young Korean men posing in high back chairs with a short biography and statement beneath their photograph. Joyce leaned over for a closer look. Some of the guys were even cute!

All through high school, Helen had refused to go on any dates, choosing to focus on her studies as Uhmma and Apa wished. Helen hung out with a close group of friends at school and then talked mostly to Su Yon at the restaurant. When Su Yon had moved away, Helen cried for days. Joyce had felt bad for Helen but didn't know how to comfort her older sister, who never before seemed fazed by anything. Joyce was already having a hard time thinking about Gina going off to a different college. She couldn't even imagine what it would be like to never talk to your best friend again.

"Now that you are getting older, it's time you started dating appropriate men," Gomo announced.

Uhmma pressed her lips together, making the skin around the edge of her mouth white. Helen had always been the obedient daughter and listened to whatever Uhmma and Apa said. If Gomo thought Helen was ready to date, then Uhmma and Apa didn't have much choice about Helen embarking on a dating odyssey.

Helen closed the book and said quietly, "Thank you, Gomo."

Joyce observed Uhmma and Apa sharing a look. Joyce wondered if they still thought Helen's studies should come first, especially with all those years of medical school still looming ahead for her.

Gomo reached down and pulled up the next shopping bag.

"This one is for Andy."

Andy jumped up and ran over to receive the bag. He even planted a kiss on Gomo's cheek. "Gam-sa-ham-nee-da, Gomo," he said and ran back to his seat with the bag.

Joyce started to get suspicious. "What's in the bag, Andy?" she asked.

Andy reached down into the bag and pulled out a large plastic container with hundreds of tiny capsules filled with a clear yellow liquid that looked like vegetable oil.

"My magic growth capsules!" Andy said and shook the container, making the pills rattle.

"What?" Joyce asked.

Gomo leaned forward. "They are shark liver extract

pills with a special Chinese root for growing taller. It was very hard to find, but I know this will make Andy happy."

Joyce turned to Andy. "Are you really going to take that?" she whispered.

Andy looked at her like she was crazy. "I asked for it, Joyce. How else am I going to make the NBA?" He gazed lovingly at his bottle of capsules. "This stuff made Tom Koh grow five inches last year."

Gomo tapped her water glass again.

"Tomorrow, I will take you to your present," Gomo said to Uhmma.

"Gomo, you did not have to do anything special for me," Uhmma said.

"This procedure will change your life," Gomo said.

Uhmma began to blink rapidly at the word *procedure*.

"What do you mean, Gomo? What procedure?"

Gomo raised her pointer finger to her eyebrows and lightly traced the shape. "Permanent makeup tattoos. I will take you to my person. She is an artist. After you get your eyebrows and eyeliner done, you will not look so tired all the time at the restaurant."

Uhmma picked up her tea and swallowed all of it in two gulps. "Gomo, really, this is much too expensive a gift for me. Please. Save your money. I do not think—"

Gomo held up her hand and stared ferociously at Uhmma until she stopped protesting.

"I will pick you up at the restaurant at two o'clock tomorrow. Surely, Mrs. Lee can handle the kitchen until you get back."

"Well. Yes." Uhmma signaled the waitress for more tea. "Yes, I believe so."

"Good." Gomo lifted her teacup to her lips, but her hawk eyes peered over the rim at Joyce.

Joyce felt her family's eyes turning to her. She pinched her chubby knees to keep from laughing nervously. The thought of all those sale clothes sounded pretty enticing right then, compared to shark liver oil, a Korean dating service, and permanent makeup tattoos. The evening was turning into a strange Korean game show with even stranger prizes.

"Joyce," Gomo said, "I have made a doctor's appointment for you. Next week, we will go and visit Dr. Rie-ne-or."

"Who?" Joyce said, still confused.

Gomo set her teacup down. She patted the corners of her lips with her napkin. "My doctor," she said. "He is Jewish. Very smart." Gomo pointed to her temple.

Joyce reached up to the zit on her temple. It had gone down a lot, but there was still a scar there from all the picking.

"Oh, for my skin," Joyce said. "It's really not that bad. I should just stop eating chocolate, but maybe seeing a dermatologist will help. Gam-sa-ham-nee-da, Gomo."

Joyce felt pleased that her gift was a practical one.

Gomo leaned forward and studied Joyce's face. "Yes, the san-gah-pu-rhee will change your entire face. Dr. Rie-ne-or will make your eyes much bigger."

Joyce glanced around the table, but none of her family members would meet her gaze. "What does a dermatologist have to do with eyes?"

Gomo turned in her seat. "Where is our banchan? They could at least bring us some kimchee." Gomo signaled the waitress.

"I don't get it." Joyce said. "I thought a dermatologist only looked at skin and stuff."

Andy leaned over. "Dr. Reiner. You know."

"Dr. Reiner?"

Andy curled his upper lip and whispered, "Dr. Reiner. Remember? Michael's plastic surgeon."

Joyce sat back in her seat. Her breath came in shallow pants. The plastic surgeon. Gomo's plastic surgeon.

Gomo turned back to the table after the waitress

left. She stared at Joyce. "The double eyelid fold surgery is a very simple procedure. It was my first operation." Gomo closed her eyes, pointed to her upper eyelids and then opened her eyes again. Twin crescent moon creases appeared above her piercing black hawk eyes. "These days, they do not even cut the skin with a knife. They use a laser and only sew a little here and there."

Joyce picked up her tea and swigged it down, wishing for once it was shoju. A knife? Laser? Just the very thought made Joyce sweat.

Gomo wiggled her finger at Joyce from across the table. "I know you want to be beautiful like Helen. You will never be as pretty as your sister, but with my doctor's help, you can look very nice."

Joyce lowered her head and raised the napkin to her mouth, wishing she could wipe more than the corners of her lips. She bit down on the inside of her cheek and furiously blinked back the tears. If nothing else, you could always count on Michael to be brutally honest.

At the end of the night, everyone stood outside of the restaurant and took their turn again to thank Gomo for her generous gifts. Gomo reminded Uhmma that she would come by tomorrow to pick her up for the appointment. Uhmma said faintly, "Yes, I'll be ready."

They waved and bowed again and watched as Gomo drove away. Apa faced his family. "Now," he said. "That was not too bad." He turned around to step off the curb, and before anyone could catch him, he somehow misplaced his step and fell down onto the street, one shoe slipping off as his ankle twisted under his weight.

Uhmma rushed to his side. "Apa, are you all right?" She tried to help him stand. "What happened?"

Apa slowly stood up with Uhmma's help, while Joyce retrieved his shoe.

As Joyce bent down to set the shoe in front of him, she noticed something odd about how it was made. She stared at his feet. At the way his one shoeless foot dangled so much farther from the ground than the foot that was planted firmly in his new wing-tip shoes. And then it all made sense.

"Apa," Joyce said, "did Gomo give you shoes with lifts in them?"

Apa smiled sheepishly. "I look taller."

Helen and Andy groaned.

"It's like you're wearing man heels." Andy laughed.

"Hey, shark liver boy," Helen said. "Look who's talking."

Uhmma sighed. "Your Gomo has her own ideas sometimes."

Apa slipped his shoe on, but he still hobbled and could not put weight on the injured foot. Helen studied him trying to walk and said, "You sprained it, Apa. You're going to have to ice it when you get home."

Uhmma helped Apa walk to the car as Helen, Andy and Joyce followed behind.

"Michael strikes again," Andy stated.

EIGHT

gina pushed open the door to the department store and waved Joyce in first. Joyce smiled at the chivalrous gesture and curtsied in response before entering. Soft jazz piano music filtered down from the escalator atrium. Joyce squinted for a second as her eyes adjusted to the bright light that seemed to radiate from every corner and counter. A floral bouquet from the perfume aisles mingled with the smell of new leather from the shoe and purse department. Joyce inhaled deeply and then sneezed three times in a row. Gina grabbed Joyce by the hand and pulled her forward into the maze of cosmetics counters.

"Try this one," Gina suggested and held up the tester tube of bright red lip gloss.

"That's too bold," Joyce protested.

"It's gloss, Joyce," Gina said with a slightly exasperated tone in her voice. "Gloss is sheer when you put it on."

"Are you sure?"

"Do I not work here part-time?"

Joyce took the tester tube and examined it closely. "You work in the stockroom."

"But I come out at every break." Gina handed Joyce a Q-tip that she magically produced from behind a mirror.

"So?" Joyce dipped the Q-tip into the tube, and applied the gloss to her lips.

Gina squinted at Joyce's lips. "So I've tried everything."

Joyce examined herself in the round mirror. "Don't you think it looks too goopy?"

Gina reached behind a makeup tray and pulled out a tissue. Joyce took it gratefully and wiped the gloss off her lips. Gina grabbed another tube of gloss and Q-tip, and stared intently at herself in the mirror as she dabbed some on.

"Why are we here, anyway?" Joyce asked.

"So you can buy me some makeup."

"What?"

Gina stood back from the mirror to check the effect of the gloss on her full lips. "You owe me for the yearbook, remember?"

Joyce slouched against the glass front of the display counter. "Oh, yeah."

"And," Gina said, studying another tube of gloss, "we can try some stuff on your eyes."

Joyce could feel her posture slipping even further. "I can't believe crazy Michael."

Gina layered another color of gloss on top of the one she was already wearing.

"What do you think?" Gina asked.

Joyce stared at her purple-lipped friend. "Too Barney."

Gina checked her reflection. "Like the dinosaur or the department store?"

Joyce chuckled. "God, only you would ask that. Dinosaur. Can we just focus on me for a second."

Gina grabbed another tissue and wiped her lips. "What are you so upset about? It's not like Michael wants to stick some double Ds in there. Although if Michael did spring for that, you know John would be looking at you differently." Gina poked Joyce in the sternum.

"Oww!" Joyce yelled. "That hurt, Gina!"

A saleswoman in her fake lab coat came over. "May I help you ladies?"

"We're just looking," Gina said and grabbed Joyce's hand again, pulling her down the aisle. The photographs of flawless models' faces peered down at them as they walked from counter to counter. Their brightly colored eyelids beckoned to Joyce. She stood before them mesmerized.

Like most Asian girls, Joyce knew about the san-gah-pu-rhee or double eyelid fold surgery, but Joyce didn't actually know anyone who had gone through with it except for Gomo, and that didn't really count. Once a few years back, when Joyce and her family had visited Korea, her cousin had showed her some magazines and said she dreamed about getting the surgery that many girls in Korea got as birthday or graduation presents. Joyce recalled being slightly curious, but waved it off as just another crazy Korean fad.

Joyce studied the poster-sized close-up of the model's face. The layers of color on her eyelids fanned out like the feathers of a peacock. Now that Joyce's attention had been drawn to this detail, she couldn't stop staring at the fold or lack of a fold in all the women she knew and met.

Gina had nice almond-shaped eyes, normal by

Korean standards, but she did not have the double eyelids that Western women took for granted. Joyce's mother had narrow creases above her eyes, and when Joyce asked about them, wondering if she had already gone through with the surgery before leaving Korea, Uhmma explained that years of applying makeup and older thin skin had naturally caused her folds to appear. Helen didn't have to worry about getting a fold like Joyce. Her eyes were so large, even without the creases, that people sometimes thought that she was Hapa or half Asian and half Caucasian, just like John Ford Kang. Joyce turned and found a mirror. Her eyes had never seemed narrow before, but as she stared at herself surrounded by the faces of countless models, the hurtful term *slant-eyes* popped into her head. Her gaze shifted back and forth from the shape of the models' eyes to her eyes. Joyce raised her fingertips to the outer edges of her eyelids. Why hadn't she noticed how thin and small they were? No wonder John mistook me for Lynn, Joyce thought.

Joyce widened her eyes, raising her eyebrows as far as they would go, and turned to Gina.

"How do I look?"

Gina glanced up from studying some facial cleansers.

"Like a scared dweeb. And your eyes aren't going to look like that after the surgery."

Joyce frowned and relaxed her eyebrows.

Gina moved on to some blushes arranged like a palette of watercolor paints. Joyce followed behind.

"You know, it's major surgery," Joyce said. "Remember last month when that woman collapsed after she got lipo? I mean, I could die."

Gina gave her a sideways glare.

"I don't know if I can go through with it, but Uhmma will kill me if I offend Gomo. And if a lot of Asian girls get this surgery, then how come we don't know anyone who did it? Maybe they had it done but didn't tell anyone. I don't want people always staring at my face and wondering what's real and what's not. What if they point and whisper behind my back? And it's gotta hurt afterwards. You know how much I hate pain. I even have to put Band-Aids on paper cuts. What if I can't see for a while? How am I going to get around? What if—"

Gina suddenly reached out and grabbed Joyce by the shoulders, giving her a good shake. "Joyce. Stop it. What are you complaining about? Damn. So many girls would be dying to be in your shoes. Your Gomo is going to PAY for you to get the fold. Come on!"

Joyce stepped back. "Would you do it?"

Gina threw up her hands. "Of course. In a heartbeat. It's free!"

Joyce pushed her hair behind her ears and turned to face her image in the mirror. "Do you think it'll make me look okay? I won't look weird and fake?"

Gina came up behind her. "You'll look like yourself only better. More alert," Gina said and widened her eyes slightly.

"I still don't know," Joyce said.

"What is so different about getting your eyes done compared to the time your Gomo paid to get your teeth fixed? I would kill to have a rich aunt fix my flaws."

Joyce ran her tongue over her perfectly aligned teeth. "I guess, but the eye-fold thing seems more extreme."

Gina made a choking noise and went back to studying the blushes. She lifted up the display box and pulled out a cotton ball.

"How did you know that was there?" Joyce wondered.

Gina blotted the cotton ball to the shell pink blush and gingerly swept it across her cheekbone. "I work here, Joyce."

Gina finally picked out two tubes of gloss and a small container of loose powder. After buying them for her, Joyce called it even.

"You owe me, now," Joyce said.

Gina smiled. "That's the way it should be. Feels good to have the natural order of our friendship restored. I was starting to get that high and mighty feeling."

Gina took Joyce's hand and pulled her forward. "Come on."

"Where are we going now?" Joyce asked.

"To get your eyes done!"

The two girls hid behind a particularly large display of potpourri, candles and paisley makeup bags. Gina picked up a bottle of perfume from the counter and sprayed some on her wrist before slowly turning around.

"There she is," Gina said, bringing her wrist up to her nose and quickly pointing in the direction of a pretty Asian woman arranging some brochures on a counter.

"She had the surgery done?"

"I don't know," Gina said, her eyes fixed on the woman. "But she sells the best makeup for Asian women and their eyes."

"Huh?" Joyce said.

"Trust me."

"Gina. Wait!" Joyce stumbled out from behind the display, trailing after her determined friend.

Gina plopped herself on one of the white terry-cloth-covered stools and motioned Joyce over to do the same. Joyce was too embarrassed to sit, so she stood next to the stool.

"Aren't these for people who pay?" Joyce whispered.

"Stop being such a worrywart," Gina scolded.

The Asian saleslady glanced in their direction and finished arranging her brochures before gliding over to them. Joyce noticed that even her walk resembled something she had seen on television. The perfect swivel in the hips, hands gracefully swinging along. Joyce made a note to herself to practice walking that way at home.

"Do you have a question, girls?"

Gina answered with a haughty voice. "My friend is looking for some eye makeup for her sister's wedding."

"Oh." The saleswoman seemed surprised that they

had a legitimate reason for being there. "When is the date?"

Gina breezed through the answer. "It's next week. We don't have a lot of time because Joyce still has to go in for her final dress fitting, but I told her that you do the best Asian eyes in the business."

The saleslady issued a charmed laugh. Gina joined in while grabbing Joyce by the back of her shirt. "She's the maid of honor," Gina said and forced Joyce to sit on the terry-cloth stool.

Joyce gulped. She hated when Gina did this. How many times had she gotten dragged into one of Gina's schemes only to have the whole thing backfire? Please, please don't ask me any questions, Joyce thought.

The saleslady carefully studied Joyce's face, lightly touching Joyce's chin when she wanted Joyce to turn her head to the left or right. She smiled at Joyce.

"Why don't I do your entire face and that way we can really make your eyes shine. My name's Arlene, by the way, if you have any questions."

Gina nudged Joyce.

"I'm Joyce."

Arlene smiled. "Well, Joyce, let's get started with a concealer for the blemishes and then a light foundation."

A sleepy feeling of well-being settled over Joyce as Arlene lightly powdered her face with a large fluffy brush. It was like the feeling she got while getting her hair washed before a haircut. It was nice having someone take care of you.

Joyce could feel Arlene's breath on her forehead as she lightly dabbed a bit more foundation around the scab at her temple.

"You really shouldn't pick," Arlene admonished.

"You sound like my mom," Joyce muttered, her eyes still closed.

"Sometimes mothers do know best. There, you can open your eyes."

Joyce slowly opened her eyes and stared into the mirror that Arlene was holding up.

"See how smooth your skin looks?" Arlene said. "Now, when we do your eyes, they are just going to pop right out from that flawless palette."

Joyce scanned the counter for Gina. "Where did my friend go?"

Arlene was rifling through her makeup drawer. "Oh, I think I saw her head over to the escalators."

Joyce clenched her jaw. She couldn't believe Gina had left her alone.

Arlene turned back to Joyce, wielding a black pencil. "Let's get started on your eyes."

Carefully, with quick, sure strokes, Arlene lined Joyce's eyes with smoky black. "You don't have a strong crease in your eyelids, so I'm going to keep the line fairly thin so that we can still get some color on your upper lids."

"What do you mean?" Joyce whispered.

Arlene stood back to survey her work before nodding. She pointed up to her own eyes. "See this?" She blinked in slow motion. The same twin crescent moons that Gomo had shown her last night appeared and disappeared each time Arlene blinked.

"Some lucky few are born with the folds, but many Asian women have to surgically create them."

"Oh." Joyce noticed that Arlene didn't say whether hers were natural or not.

Arlene came back with a small compact and showed her the colors of the eye shadow. "What colors did your sister pick for your bridesmaid gown?"

"Huh?" Joyce said.

Arlene smiled patiently. "The color theme. I thought maybe I could complement it with your eye shadow color."

Joyce still had no idea what Arlene was talking about, but she picked two colors anyway. "Uhm, I think purple and green."

Arlene looked surprised. "That's kind of different." She studied the eye shadow palette in her hands and pursed her lips. "Maybe this velvet brown might work."

Joyce closed her eyes as she saw Arlene reaching forward with her small angled brush.

"Did your sister hire a wedding consultant?"

"Yeah," Joyce said quickly.

Arlene spoke more to herself. "I wonder who she went with, because the colors are so unusual." Arlene pulled back. "She didn't go with someone from the Valley, did she?"

Joyce tried to look as horrified as Arlene. "Oh, no."

"I suppose purple and green could look really sophisticated, depending on the shade."

"Yeah," Joyce quickly agreed and started to sneeze again.

Arlene handed her a tissue.

"I'm going to start with the darker colors near your eyes and lighten as we get closer to your eyebrows. Most Asians can't wear more than two or three shades because of the size of their fold." Arlene stood back to check her work and then brought the brush for a final dusting on Joyce's lids. Joyce wanted to ask Arlene about the surgery. Maybe she knew people who had come to her afterwards for some makeup tips. Maybe Arlene had undergone plastic surgery. Joyce crossed her legs, uncrossed them, and crossed them again. There was only one way to find out, and her makeup session was almost over.

"Now for your lip color," Arlene said and reached back for a small rectangular tray that held an assortment of lipstick shades. "I would suggest going with something a little bolder than what you are probably used to. See this color?" Arlene pointed it out.

"Can I ask you a question, Arlene?" Joyce interrupted.

Arlene looked up.

Joyce stared at Arlene's perfectly creased lids. "Have you ever had plastic surgery?"

A tiny line appeared between Arlene's eyebrows. "Did someone put you up to this?" she asked.

"No!" Joyce frantically shook her head. "Oh, no. No, not at all."

Arlene stepped back and evaluated Joyce, but

this time, she seemed to be looking at Joyce's eyes as opposed to her entire face. Arlene's eyes narrowed. "Did you hear something about me?"

Joyce could feel her face flaming up under all the makeup. Joyce's hands began to flutter. "No, I didn't even know you worked here until my friend Gina brought me over to your counter. I was just curious."

"Well, maybe you should learn to mind your own business."

"I'm sorry. I didn't mean to pry. It's just that. Oh, man." Joyce's face itched like crazy, but she knew she couldn't damage all the work that Arlene had just done. Joyce reached up and scratched the top of her head. "I don't know what I'm doing here. Well, I do know, but it's kind of weird. It's like this. My aunt offered to give me that eyelid surgery. You know, to get the folds put in."

Arlene raised one eyebrow.

"Really," Joyce continued. "And I'm not sure if I should get them, but my friend Gina thought that if I got a makeover I might see how good I could look. That, and I owed her money for a yearbook and I had to pay her back and she wanted—"

Arlene lightly touched Joyce's shoulders. "Joyce, you are babbling. Plastic surgery isn't something you should jump into because you're getting it as a gift." Arlene stepped closer to Joyce and nodded in time to her lecture. "Accidents can happen. Painful, unforeseeable events that can change your whole life and the way you feel. Even the best doctors can't always anticipate the way your skin will react or heal after the surgery."

Joyce gulped. "Oh."

Arlene stepped back. "Now, if you go with this color for your lips, your eyes will look even more luminous." Without even waiting for an answer, Arlene lightly applied the lipstick to Joyce's lips and then layered it with some gloss. "There," Arlene said and swiveled Joyce around.

Joyce stared at herself in the large display mirror. It was her and not her. She could feel the layers of makeup like a film of plastic over her skin. Her lips were plump and shiny red as a new car. The smooth plateau of her cheeks, dewy and flawless, glowed with a pearlescent sheen. And her eyes! Joyce leaned in closer. Her eyes were lightly outlined in black with gradations of smoky browns on her upper lids. Joyce's eyes definitely looked bigger. They smoldered with an intensity that Joyce couldn't believe was coming from her. She scowled and found her image mimicking her.

"I can't believe that's me!" Joyce said.

Arlene crossed her arms. "All this without one cut or stitch. And there's no recovery time."

"Yeah," Joyce said and shifted her weight on the stool, painfully aware of sitting still for all that time.

Arlene began arranging the products she had used on the counter. "Now, for the wedding, you'll want to make sure to layer a little more gloss on your lips, especially if you are going to be taking pictures right after the ceremony."

"Uhm, Arlene," Joyce said, hopping off the stool.

Arlene turned around. She saw Joyce standing awkwardly by the stool.

"About my sister's wedding."

Arlene leaned her weight back and rested her elbows on the counter. "There isn't a wedding."

Joyce nodded.

"I thought purple and green sounded pretty suspicious, but then those are the kinds of colors people are picking these days. Always trying to be different and original. I thought I was getting old for a second."

"Oh, no," Joyce said. "You don't look old at all."

Arlene's lips twitched. "Thanks, honey."

Joyce slowly backed away. "I love what you did to my face. And if I had money I would buy all of it. Really, I would. But I just paid back my friend Gina, the one who was here a minute ago. I just wanted to see what my eyes could look like."

Arlene waved her away. "Just be careful and make sure to research your doctor. Get references and check them out."

Joyce nodded.

"Remember, there's always makeup!"

Joyce waved and headed over to the escalators. She was going to kill Gina. Right after Gina had finished admiring Joyce's amazing makeover.

N I N E

all the way home, Joyce had to fight the inclination to touch her face. Gina, even while driving her mother's car, could see Joyce's hand go up and she would reach out and swat Joyce's fingers away.

"Joyce, you'll ruin it."

"But it itches!" Joyce scratched her neck, which was as close to the real itch as she could get.

"You look fabulous. At least five years older. Don't you want people to see?" Gina asked.

"I feel like I'm drowning." Joyce checked her fingernails. "Gross, look at all that makeup." She held out her hand for Gina to see the foundation caked under her nails.

Gina continued staring forward. She said three words. "John Ford Kang."

Joyce stopped studying her nails and slouched back into her seat.

At a red light, Gina shifted around and faced Joyce. "Do you want him to mistake you for Lynn again next year?"

"No."

"Then stop acting like a child."

Joyce tried not to pout. "I'm just not used to wearing this much foundation."

Gina rolled her eyes and sped up as the light turned green. Gina dropped Joyce off in front of her apartment complex.

"Promise you won't wash it off and you'll go to work with it on?" Gina asked.

Joyce groaned. "No way."

"Come on, Joyce. You said it yourself, you have to get used to wearing the makeup. Everyone is going to say how great you look."

"You think so?"

"Yes!"

Joyce sighed deeply to let Gina know how much it hurt. "Fine."

Gina clapped. "Good. I'll come by the restaurant later tonight."

"Where are you going now?" Joyce asked.

"I have to go by the Korean market and then I'm just gonna take more SAT practice tests until I have to pick up my mom."

"Everyone has a car," Joyce said and pushed open her door.

"It's not that glamorous, Joyce," Gina called out as Joyce stepped out.

Joyce waved good-bye and headed into her apartment complex. As she walked up the stairs, Joyce assessed her wardrobe. What could she wear to work to go with her new makeover? She had it narrowed down to two shirts by the time she reached her front door. Joyce was just about to push her key into the lock when she realized the door was slightly ajar. Did she forgot to lock up before leaving the apartment? Had there been a break-in? Joyce slowly pushed open the front door, her breath shallow with fear.

Uhmma was sitting on the couch, her back to the door.

"Uhmma?" Joyce said, surprised to see her mother home.

Uhmma slowly turned her head at the sound of Joyce's voice.

Joyce quickly covered her mouth, squelching the scream of horror.

Where Uhmma's head should have been, there was an enormous balloon. Her eyes were replaced by two slight indentations, like tucks in a down ski jacket. Her bulging forehead, the skin shiny and taut from swelling, cast a shadow over her puffed-out cheeks. Two dark lines where her eyebrows used to be glowered back at Joyce, evil as a jack-o'-lantern. Joyce had never seen anything like it before. Uhmma looked like she had just walked off the set of a horror movie or, worse, a late-night comedy show. But instead of a conehead, she had a Nerf-ball head.

"Uhmma, are you okay? What happened?" Joyce asked, peering back and forth, searching for Uhmma's eyes.

Two fat tears slid out from under the tucks.

"Don't cry, Uhmma!" Joyce said, alarmed. She grabbed Uhmma's hands, which were thankfully normal sized, and patted them.

Uhmma's puffy lips parted. "Gomo."

"They did this to you at the permanent makeup place?"

Uhmma shook her head no and pointed to the dark lines on her forehead. "They tattooed my eyebrows, and on the way home, my face blew up."

Joyce stood up. "Ohmygod! We have to get you to the hospital." Joyce wondered if they could just pop Uhmma's head like deflating a balloon.

Uhmma shook her head again. "Helen already took me. I am supposed to rest and take the medicine." She pointed to a bottle of pills on the coffee table. "The doctors say I had some allergic reaction to the tattoo ink."

Joyce sat back down next to Uhmma. Arlene's words rang in her ears. Joyce reached up to her own face and felt the stiffness of the foundation and powder like armor on her skin. At least this stuff could be washed off.

"Does it hurt?" Joyce asked.

Two more tears slid out.

Joyce gently wiped them away. "Do you want some water? Can you eat something?"

"Don't worry about me. Go help your father at work. Mrs. Lee cannot do everything. Also, ask Gina to come and help tonight. Helen will have to work in the kitchen."

Joyce nodded.

Uhmma sighed. "I had a dream something like this would happen. Aigoo. Your Gomo sometimes makes me crazy."

"She's crazy, Uhmma."

Uhmma waved away her comment. "Shhh, do not be disrespectful. Gomo does so much for us."

Joyce turned away. How many times had she heard the same thing? Gomo was their savior. Jesus! Gomo could seriously maim them all and they would still have to bow and say gam-sa-ham-nee-da.

"It's ridiculous that we have to kiss up to her all the time," Joyce said.

"Joyce-ya, you do not understand. We can never repay her for all her help. Without Gomo we would not even be here. We would not even own our restaurant. We must take care of her now in her old age. This is the Korean way."

Joyce sighed. "I know, I know, Uhmma."

Uhmma reached for Joyce's shoulder, but overshot the mark and poked Joyce in the eye. "Be nice, Joyce."

Joyce held her injured eye and slouched forward.

The whole idea of getting the folds was starting to feel scary. If this could happen to Uhmma just from a tattoo, then who knew what could happen on the operating table. What if her eyes became deformed, all for the sake of vanity? Not to mention all the pain. "Uhmma, do I have to get the san-gah-pu-rhee?"

"You do not want to?"

Joyce shrugged and then remembered Uhmma couldn't see her. "I don't know."

Uhmma leaned back into the couch. "You might like it," Uhmma said weakly.

"Maybe," Joyce said, remembering Gomo's comment about how she could never be as pretty as Helen.

"It is hard to say no to Gomo," Uhmma said. "But if you do not want the surgery, we will find a way to say no."

Joyce turned to Uhmma. "Really?"

Uhmma nodded and two more tears slid out. "My daughters should not be unhappy."

"Helen doesn't like her gift? What's so wrong with dating? It's not like she has to marry them," Joyce complained.

"Joyce-ya, please. You are too hard on Helen. She has a lot on her mind these days," Uhmma said.

"Helen's always too busy."

Uhmma reached out and grabbed Joyce's shoulder, this time making contact. "Joyce, you must be more understanding of your older sister. She is your uhn-nee and she tries her best to be good to you."

Joyce rolled her eyes, knowing Uhmma couldn't see her reaction.

"Fine," Joyce said to stop the lecture.

Uhmma reached over to pat Joyce's knee and ended up comforting the pillow on the sofa.

Joyce left Uhmma with the television on even though she couldn't see it; at least her hearing wasn't affected by the swelling. She walked into the bathroom to wash off all the makeup. Joyce stared at herself in the mirror as she waited for the hot water to start running. It had to be easier to be a boy. She cupped the warm water in her hands and plunged in her face.

As Joyce made her way down the outside stairs to the bike rack, she saw Sam coming out of his apartment. He automatically raised the camera to his face and began taking pictures.

"Hey, Sam," Joyce said and waved furiously at the camera, her hand blocking her face.

"How am I supposed to take a picture of you?" Sam asked.

"Exactly," Joyce said as she got to the bottom of the stairs.

Sam lowered his camera. "Everything okay with your mom?"

Joyce sighed. "You heard?"

Sam nodded as he fiddled with his camera settings.

"She's okay, but I don't think she'll want to go out in public for a while. Her face is pretty bad."

Sam raised the camera to his face and began shooting at some of the plants outlining the filled-in pool area.

"I miss the pool," Joyce said, trying to change the subject. It was always hard to talk about appearances with Sam, even though he was a photographer. Half the time when he was taking pictures, it seemed more like he was trying to hide behind the camera. Sam had a type of acne that haunted teenagers in their worst nightmares. Deep cystic swells made his face purple and misshapen. The deep craterlike scars on his cheeks made it hard not to stare. Uhmma always said that acne was a rite of passage. Something you only had to endure through your teen years. Sam was enduring and then some. Luckily, he seemed to be growing out of them; the cysts seemed to be shrinking. Joyce thought about what she would have done if her acne were as bad as Sam's. If Gomo had offered to fix something like that, Joyce would not have had to think twice about accepting.

"It's all about the cost in the end," Sam said, clicking off a couple more shots.

"Huh?" Joyce said.

Sam pointed at the pool area. "Pools cost a lot to maintain, not to mention the insurance on something like that."

"How do you know all this?" Joyce asked.

Sam smiled and raised his camera to his face again, firing off another shot of Joyce. "I know a lot of useless information."

"Do you know how to pop a human balloon head?" Joyce asked.

"Was all the swelling from just the eyebrow tattoos?" Sam asked, lowering his camera.

"Korean mothers' grapevine still working like a charm," Joyce said.

Sam shrugged. It was hard to keep anything a secret in the Korean community, let alone the apartment complex, which housed four Korean families.

"My mom got those eyebrow tattoos last year," Sam said quietly.

"Really? And she didn't have any kind of reaction?"

Sam shook his head. "Nah. It was like a party. She and my aunts all went together and got their eyebrows and eyeliner done."

Joyce was shocked. How many of these Korean women were walking around with permanent makeup on? "That is so weird," Joyce said.

Sam gazed down at the ground and smiled. "Yeah, tell me about it. In the mornings my mom looks like she just got back from some goth club or something. She says it cuts down on the amount of time it takes every day to make herself presentable."

Joyce grinned thinking about how long she had to sit while Arlene applied the makeup to her face. "I could see the point."

Sam quickly glanced up at her to see if she was joking. His large brown eyes crinkled up in a question. No fold, Joyce noticed.

"I have to get to the restaurant," Joyce said and headed toward the bike rack. "We have a lot of work to do without Uhmma around."

Sam followed after her. "Do you need a ride? I have the car tonight."

Joyce whirled around. "Why does everyone have a car except for me?"

"Huh?"

"Nothing," Joyce said. She stared at her bike. "Yeah, sure. I could use a break from my bike."

Sam was a confident driver, one hand on the steering wheel, glancing at her occasionally as they talked. Joyce had never spent much time alone with him before. Sometimes they chatted if they caught each other outside of the apartment or hung out in a larger group after church. But most of the time, Sam was a loner.

"Are you doing anything for the summer?" Sam asked, quickly checking his rearview mirror before passing a slower car.

"Nah, just working at the restaurant." Joyce glanced over at him. It was strange to be with him without his camera hovering in front of his face. His cheeks seemed particularly dry and flaky. Joyce knew from experience that benzoyl peroxide could be really harsh on the skin. She wanted to tell him about this noncomedogenic lotion she put on at night to help with the peeling, but one, it was embarrassing that she even knew the term, and two, it felt too forward. Maybe another time.

"Are you doing anything this summer?" Joyce asked.

Sam shrugged and then the right corner of his lip

turned up slightly. "I got a show in a month at this gallery."

"That is awesome, Sam!"

"It's nothing."

"Don't say that," Joyce said and playfully swatted his arm. "Where is it? Can Gina and I come?"

"Yeah," Sam quickly glanced at her and then refocused on the road. "But, really, it's not that big a deal. I'm part of this group that's showing."

"I think it's great that you are putting your work out there." Joyce pulled her legs up and wrapped her arms around them. "I have no clue what I'm going to do after high school."

Sam frowned. "You're not going to college?"

"I'm not that crazy." Joyce laughed. "My parents would kill me if I didn't at least go to some state school. I just mean I don't know what I want to study or do."

"Why do you have to know anything now?"

Joyce rested her chin on her knees. "Well, when you have a genius sister who's known she's going to be a doctor since she was eight, it's pretty hard not to be compared. And somehow," Joyce said softly, "I always end up feeling lame."

"You're not lame. You just haven't found yourself yet."

"What do you mean?"

"The first time I raised a camera to my face and looked through the lens, I realized it was okay for me to be me. I'm an outsider, an observer. I've come to accept that about myself because it makes me a better photographer. Not that I don't want friends or anything, but that's not what defines me. You know?"

Joyce wasn't sure if she did understand, but what Sam was saying had an essence that felt true. What defines me? Joyce wondered.

"I think some people just find themselves early, and other people have a longer journey." Sam licked his lips, which were looking red and parched.

"Do you want some Chap Stick?" Joyce offered, reaching down for her backpack.

Sam flushed red. He pressed his lips together for a second as though to hide them. "Nah, I'm okay. Do I turn left here?"

Joyce craned her neck to see where they were. "Uhm, no. It's the next complex. They all look alike, don't they?"

"Yeah. Sort of."

Joyce pointed ahead. "Turn left there."

Sam put on his left blinker and then eased the car into the parking lot.

"You can just drop me in front." Joyce sat up

straighter. She could see Andy running from the front dining room to the back kitchen. If even Andy was rushing around, it was going to be a tough night without Uhmma. Joyce dreaded starting work.

Sam pulled into a spot in front of the restaurant. "My mom's pointed your restaurant out before, but I've never eaten here."

"Really?" Joyce said, picking up her backpack. "Do you go to Mrs. Shin's place?"

"Yeah," Sam said sheepishly. "She's like my second cousin or something. I don't quite understand the connection. You know how it is."

Joyce nodded. Everyone was somehow related to everyone else in this town.

"Thanks, Sam," Joyce said, turning in her seat.

"No problem. It was a good excuse to use the car."

"No, I mean about what you said."

Sam shrugged. "Don't be so hard on yourself. You'll figure it out."

"Do you want to come in for a bite to eat?" Joyce asked. "It won't be fancy because my mom's out, but I can make you a mean bi-bim bop."

Sam paused for a second and then cut the engine. "Okay." He reached around to the backseat and grabbed his camera.

They walked into the restaurant and immediately heard Andy screaming from the back. "I can't be seen this way!"

Joyce tried to laugh it off. "My crazy brother having a crisis again."

Sam smiled and raised the camera to his face. "Can I take some pictures?"

"Sure," Joyce said and pointed to one of the booths. "And you can have a seat over there after you're done. I'll be right back."

Joyce walked into the kitchen to find Apa standing at the rear bathroom door and Mrs. Lee furiously chopping some scallions. Helen was nowhere to be seen.

"What's going on?" Joyce asked.

Mrs. Lee waved her knife at Apa. Apa gestured at the door. Andy cracked open the door at the sound of Joyce's voice.

"Help me, Joyce," Andy cried.

Joyce walked over. "Can you come out?"

"I can't," he said.

Apa whispered, "He had an accident."

"I did not!" Andy protested.

"Well, then, just come out so I can help you," Joyce said.

"Promise you won't laugh?" he asked.

Joyce nodded. Andy slowly emerged from the bathroom. He stood in front of her, and then, step by tiny step, he turned around. The entire seat of his khaki pants was covered with a strange, dark yellow mustard stain that immediately made Joyce cover her mouth with her hands.

"Andy, that is so nasty!"

Andy moaned. "It's not what you think it is. I didn't poop in my pants. Honest to god! I'm leaking or something, and my stomach feels really funny."

"What? Your stomach? What have you been eating today?" Joyce asked.

Andy turned back around, his eyes wide with horror.

"The shark liver pills!"

michael's poisoned me!" Andy moaned, clutching the door to the bathroom as though he would die any minute.

"Oh, stop being so melodramatic," Joyce said. She stared at Andy's pants. "Well, you'll just have to go home and change your clothes."

Apa shook his head. "Helen is not here yet, and there is a large party coming for dinner in a half hour."

"When is Helen getting here?" Joyce asked.

Apa looked at his watch. "Not for another hour."

"I cannot get everything ready in time!" Mrs. Lee called out.

Apa hobbled over to Mrs. Lee. "It is all right, Mrs. Lee. I will help you."

"No, no, Mr. Park. You should be resting your foot."

"Someone has to take me home!" Andy wailed.

"Don't touch anything," Joyce ordered Andy, throwing him a couple of aprons. "Get in the bathroom and don't come out. When Helen gets here, she can take you home."

Andy encased himself in red and blue aprons, wearing one in the front and one in the back. As he closed the bathroom door, he yelled, "Don't tell Juan anything about what happened!"

Joyce ran from the kitchen to the cash register counter and picked up the phone. She dialed Gina's number, and as she waited for Gina to pick up, she spotted Sam sitting at the booth. "Sorry, Sam. We're having a family crisis."

Gina's answering machine picked up.

Joyce left Gina a message. "Hey, get over to the restaurant as soon as you can. It's an emergency."

"Can I do anything to help?" Sam asked, walking over.

Joyce put the phone down. "Everyone in my family is either injured, sick or missing."

"That doesn't sound good," Sam said.

Joyce cradled her head in her hands for a minute while she tried to think of what to do. Apa was useless in the kitchen with his sprained ankle. It would be better if he just sat at the register. Andy was out of commission. Basically, there was Joyce and Mrs. Lee. Where was Helen? Why couldn't they call Helen to get her butt to the restaurant? She picked up the phone and dialed Helen's cell number. It immediately dropped into her voice mail. Joyce slammed down the phone.

"You sure I can't help?"

Joyce studied Sam. "Have you ever waited on tables before?"

"Nooooo," Sam said, stepping backwards. "I meant helping in a little way. Give someone a ride. Maybe wash dishes. I can't wait on tables, Joyce."

Joyce ran out from behind the counter. "Please, Sam. Just for a little while until my sister, Helen, gets here and then you can take my brother home."

"I can't do it, Joyce," Sam said, his arms crossed in front.

"Please, Sam," Joyce begged. "Please, please, please. I'll do anything."

Sam stepped back. "Anything?" he asked, giving her the photographer's squint.

"Well, not anything. There are certain clothing parameters," Joyce said.

"Hey, whoa, wait a minute. What kind of photographer do you think I am? Joyce, get your mind out of the gutter."

Joyce tried not to look so worried.

"Don't worry. I'm not working on those kinds of photos. But I would like to get some head shots." Sam chuckled at Joyce's horrified expression. "Pictures of your face."

Joyce smiled. "So you'll wait on tables?" she asked.

Sam looked away, his hands fiddling with the lens cap on his camera. Joyce made quiet mewing please-pleasepleaseplease sounds.

Sam removed the camera strap from around his neck and set the camera on the counter. "Okay."

By the time the dinner party started to arrive, Sam was armed with his pad, pen and red and blue Arirang apron. Apa sat at the register, his black-and-blue swollen ankle elevated on two pillows, calling out directions to Sam.

"Just write down whatever they say and we'll figure out the rest. Also, you can ask my apa if you have any questions," Joyce said, racing back to the kitchen.

Mrs. Lee worked the stove and grill and Joyce prepped the banchan and cut vegetables and anything else that Mrs. Lee needed for the orders.

Sam walked into the kitchen, studying what he had written down on his pad. He called out all the dishes, several of which were special orders with slight changes.

"And someone wants their order of bulgoki without any scallions," Sam said.

"Just that one order?" Joyce asked. "The rest want the scallions?"

Sam nodded. "Yeah, it's just that one order."

"Are you okay out there?" Joyce asked, handing him a tray with banchan.

He shoved the pad into the front pocket of his apron and took the tray from Joyce.

"I think it's going fine," Sam said, his eyes focused on the large tray. He gripped it tightly with both hands and slowly turned around to make his way out of the kitchen. "At least I haven't dropped anything yet," he tossed over his shoulder as he walked out.

Juan arrived at his usual time and took his spot at the large sink.

"Andy? ¿Dónde está?" Juan asked as Joyce ran frantically back and forth in the kitchen trying to locate all of the ingredients for some of the special dishes the party had ordered.

Joyce pointed to the bathroom and shrugged her shoulders.

"I can't find the chili powder," Joyce wailed to Mrs. Lee.

Mrs. Lee pointed her tongs in the air. "On the shelf above the refrigerator."

Joyce looked up. "You would think that the most used spice in this kitchen would be more accessible." She grabbed a chair and pulled it over to the refrigerator.

Mrs. Lee ignored her commentary, focusing on the sizzling meat on the grill.

Joyce jumped on the chair and reached up for the clear plastic bag that was just beyond her fingers. She raised herself up on tiptoes and stretched.

"Don't fall," Gina said.

Joyce turned around to see Gina holding the back of the chair. "Thank God you're here," Joyce cried.

"Yeah, well. I'm not the only one. Did you see who's in your dinner party?"

Joyce turned back around to try for the chili powder again. "I haven't even had a chance to breathe." She could just barely touch the edge of the bag with her middle fingers. She nudged it closer. And closer.

"John Ford Kang."

Just as Joyce grabbed the bag with both hands, the name cleared her ears and pierced into her consciousness.

"What!" Joyce yelled and quickly swiveled around, holding the bag of chili powder high above her head, her sweaty hands shaking in fear and excitement.

Mrs. Lee looked up from the grill. "The bag—" she called out just as Joyce lost her balance and jumped off the chair. A puff of chili powder rained down on her.

"Is open," Mrs. Lee said.

"MY EYES!" Joyce dropped the bag on the ground and reached up to her face.

Gina rushed Joyce to the sink.

"Oh, God, it burns, it burns," Joyce moaned and leaned over the sink. Warm water bathed her face. Joyce rubbed her eyes, but it only made the burning worse. "It's not working!"

"Keep your eyes closed and wash your face with soap!" Gina yelled and handed Joyce a bar of soap.

Joyce washed her face and then let the cold water run over her eyes. Finally, she stepped back from the sink. Gina handed her a clean dishcloth. Joyce patted her eyes dry, making sure to keep them closed. After a minute, when the threat of the burning had receded, Joyce carefully, millimeter by millimeter, parted her lids. Tears gushed out.

"Are you okay?" Gina asked.

Joyce raised her hands to brush the tears away.

"*¡Un momento!*" Juan called out to Joyce. He waved Joyce over to the sink and gestured that she should wash her hands and arms again.

Joyce nodded and Juan turned on the sprayer so that Joyce could wash off any trace of the fine chili powder.

"I didn't know his name was going to cause such a reaction," Gina said.

"That was so painful," Joyce said. She reached up to her cheeks and brushed aside the tears. Her eyes kept welling up, trying to flush out whatever remnants of the chili powder were left. "*Gracias,* Juan," Joyce said.

Juan tried to suppress his grin. "*Muy caliente,*" he said and licked his finger and touched the air hissing, pretending Joyce was on fire.

Joyce stared down at her drenched clothing. Her wet hair clung to her cheeks. And the tears would not stop. "What am I going to do? Are you sure it's JFK out there?"

Gina nodded.

"How am I going to face him looking like this?"

"Well, at least the mascara is waterproof," Gina said and then leaned in closer for an inspection. "Unless someone already washed it off."

Joyce stepped back from Gina's harsh glare. "I couldn't take the itching anymore."

Gina threw up her hands. "Joyce, what is the point?"

Mrs. Lee yelled, "I still need the chili powder!"

Gina walked over and picked up the bag off the floor and brought it to her mom. Joyce took the opportunity to run to the bathroom. The door was still closed. Joyce banged on it with her fist.

"Let me in, Andy."

"No."

"Andy, if you don't open the door, I'm going to scream that you pooped in your pants."

The door opened.

Joyce walked in. Andy sat back down on the toilet, still encased in the aprons.

"What happened out there?" Andy asked.

Joyce ignored him and checked her reflection in the mirror. Her eyes were puffy and red as though she had a bad case of hay fever. And her hair was a sopping wet mess.

Why had she washed off all that makeup? Of all the times that she needed her face on, as they said. Joyce groaned. She was starting to sound like all the other Korean women. Maybe there was something to all this makeup, glamour stuff. It was like armor in a way. Like wearing a mask or going into character. Joyce thought about how confident she felt walking through the department store after her makeover. Maybe getting her eyes done would make her look better. It certainly couldn't make her look worse. Was that a zit? Joyce leaned forward to examine the tiny bump on her chin. She gave it a hard squeeze, pressing her fingernails just to the outer edges of the raised dot.

"Don't pick, Joyce."

Joyce froze. How had she forgotten about Andy? Joyce glanced over at Andy sitting in a depressed slump. "I wasn't picking," she said.

Andy rolled his eyes.

Joyce turned around and opened the door.

"When is someone going to take me home?" Andy whimpered.

"That is the least of my worries, Andy."

Gina was helping her mom when Joyce stepped out of the bathroom. Sam rushed into the kitchen with his empty tray.

"They want their order of ji-geh right now!"

Gina grabbed a ladle and reached for the large stew pot at the back of the stove.

Sam waited with his tray out. Joyce walked over to

the doorway between the kitchen and the front dining room and snuck a peek. The group of eight sat at the large table in the corner. Even with his back to her and her eyes still burning, Joyce could spot John Ford Kang from across the room. The perfect triangle of his shoulders narrowed down to his waist. The longish brown hair curling just at the edges over the collar of his T-shirt. His chiseled triceps accentuated by the tight band of fabric on his short sleeves. Joyce grabbed the edge of the door frame.

"It's him," Joyce said and turned around.

Gina was setting the clay bowl on the tray Sam held out. Gina looked up. "Did you doubt my powers of identification?"

Sam kept his eyes on the bowl of spicy stew, his knuckles white with the effort of holding the tray. Slowly he turned around to take the stew out to the dining room.

"Whoever he is, they're definitely on the demanding side," Sam said before carefully walking out with the ji-geh.

"What am I going to do?" Joyce asked, her eyes on Sam as he took slow, tiny steps toward the table.

Gina walked up behind Joyce. "Just go out there and say, Hey, you're eating at my restaurant."

Joyce turned to her. "Look at me! Do I look ready to face him?"

"You would if you hadn't washed off all that makeup!"

Joyce rubbed the rest of the tears from her eyes. "It wouldn't have mattered anyway with that chili powder fiasco."

"I guess," Gina sighed. "Well, you can still go and introduce yourself to him and his family."

Sam made it all the way to the table without spilling a drop. He set the stew down in front of an elderly woman who could have been John's grandmother and then walked back to the kitchen.

"Who is that guy?" Sam asked as he entered the kitchen and set down his tray on the prep table.

"Some guy from school that has Joyce all hot and bothered," Gina said.

Joyce began to pace and mumble, "What am I going to do? What am I going to say? I haven't practiced for this."

Andy poked his head out of the bathroom. "Jeez, would you stop obsessing already and go out there."

Joyce glowered at him and pointed her finger. "Back inside, poopy pants."

Andy stuck his tongue out before shutting the door.

"Joyce," Gina said, "you just have to put some ice on your eyes and dry your hair and then you'll look fine."

Joyce reached up to her wet hair. "Really? You think so?"

Gina walked over to the freezer and pulled out a bag of frozen peas. She threw them over to Joyce and then walked over to the stove. "Look, we'll turn the stove on high and you can kind of stand near it and I'll wave the heat over to—"

Sam stepped forward, his hands waving back and forth. "Hold up, do I have to be the voice of reason here? What if your hair catches on fire?"

Gina turned on the burner. Mrs. Lee stood at the prep table, her back to the girls, her knife flying through the vegetables as she frantically prepared the rest of the banchan for the dinner rush that would begin in another hour.

"Come on, Joyce, this is your chance. You can finally get him to recognize you."

Joyce stood there, holding the peas, trying to decide what to do.

"Don't do it, Joyce," Sam said quietly.

Joyce began gnawing at the webbing of skin between her thumb and pointer finger, trying to make a decision.

"John Ford Kang," Gina said.

As though hypnotized, Joyce shuffled over to the stove. A blast of heat rose up and hit her face. Gina lifted up a large clump of hair stuck to Joyce's cheek, making sure the flames weren't too close.

Sam untied the apron from around his waist and dropped it on the table. "I guess, Joyce, you don't need my help anymore." He knocked on the bathroom door. "Let's go home, Andy."

"Finally," Andy said and emerged from the bathroom.

"Thanks for everything, Sam," Joyce called out as Sam and Andy left the kitchen through the back alley door.

"Is it drying?" Joyce asked Gina.

"It's working," Gina said. "Put the peas over your eyes."

Joyce reached up, and surprisingly, her hair was dryer than before. She glanced over at Juan, who was standing at the dishwasher watching them, his eyebrows knotted in concern. When he caught Joyce's eyes, he licked his finger and touched the air, hissing his worries. Joyce smiled and nodded her head. *Muy caliente.* Joyce tipped her head back a bit and placed the bag of frozen peas over her eyes.

Just as Gina was finishing up, Joyce could hear someone entering the kitchen from the back door.

"What are you two doing?" Helen asked.

"None of your business," Joyce said, her eyes still covered. "Why was your cell phone turned off?"

Helen groaned. "Oh, no, I'm sorry. I meant to turn it back on after the meeting."

"Well, while you were doing other things, we were in crisis mode," Joyce said, removing the peas and stepping toward Helen. Gina grabbed the ends of Joyce's hair and yanked her back.

"Just another second," Gina said, wafting the hot air over to Joyce.

"What happened?" Helen asked, setting her bags down in the storage room.

"Andy got sick from the shark liver pills, and there was no one to cover the front, and there was a massive dinner party that came in early."

Helen tied an apron around her waist. "But Apa said it was going to be quiet until later in the evening. There wasn't a dinner party on the books."

"Yeah, well, nothing went as planned today, and you weren't around."

Helen pulled her hair back into a ponytail. "Look, Joyce, I'm sorry you couldn't get a hold of me. I'm here now. I'll take care of the dinner party while you and Gina do whatever to your hair. And if it was as crazy as you said it was, I don't know how doing your hair over the stove is any way to deal with it."

Joyce narrowed her eyes. "Just do me a favor and shut up."

Helen walked out of the kitchen.

"Come on, Gina. My hair doesn't have to be completely dry."

"Okay, okay," Gina said and released Joyce.

"How do I look?" Joyce asked and stepped away from the stove.

Gina studied Joyce's eyes for a second and then raised her thumb. "Perfectly presentable."

"Presentable? What does that mean?" Joyce worried.

Gina gave her a slight push. "Stop overanalyzing. Just go out there before he leaves."

Joyce took a deep breath and walked over to the doorway.

Helen and John were exchanging hugs at the front door. They were too far away for Joyce to eavesdrop, but Joyce could see John's father studying Helen's face as John pointed to Helen and waved his hands emphatically in the air. Helen smiled faintly, looking embarrassed. As John's father pushed open the glass door to leave, Helen bowed, her hands clasped in front. John waved, following his father out of the restaurant. The rest of the group also bowed and quickly filed out.

Joyce turned around in a daze. Gina looked up from helping her mother and immediately ran over.

"What happened? I thought you were going out there," Gina said, putting one arm around Joyce's shoulders.

"I hate her," Joyce stated and fell into Gina's arms.

ELEVEN

joyce and Gina sat on a large sack of rice in the storage room. The two had retreated from the kitchen, trying to make sense of how Helen and John knew each other.

"Are you sure they hugged?" Gina asked again.

Joyce stared miserably at the cement floor. "Yes."

Gina shook her head. "But wouldn't you have known if Helen was friends with John?"

Joyce sniffled. "Let's please stop talking about it. I don't care how they know each other. They obviously do, and once again, I am second in line. Why would John ever want to go out with me if he knows Helen?" Joyce stared up at the fluorescent lights. "I hate being the ugly sister."

Gina came rushing to her defense. "Whoa, wait. Stop harshing on yourself. Who said you're the ugly sister? Come on, Joyce."

Joyce frowned. "Let's face it. It's true. Helen's always been prettier and better at everything."

Gina stood up, silent.

"See, even you aren't going to argue with me about that," Joyce wailed.

Gina whirled around. "No, that's not true, Joyce. I mean, I don't believe Helen's better than you at everything," Gina said, her eyes scanning the room. "I'm just trying to find something."

Gina leaped over to the shelves and picked up a large white dish towel. She folded it into a triangle and placed it over her hair, knotting the two ends under her chin.

Joyce stared at Gina, who now resembled a sweet country girl working in the fields.

Gina pointed into the air. "Look, it's Godzilla!"

Joyce refused to smile, deepening her frown. Gina widened her eyes and made her mouth into a large O. "Oh, no, he is crushing our house!"

Joyce began to crack, the corners of her lips quivering.

Gina glanced at her and then began to hop around

the tiny room, patting her full cheeks. "Please, please, save me."

Joyce broke into a grin that deepened until she began to laugh.

"Godzilla, do not eat me! Ahhhhh!" Gina crumbled to the ground in a grand faint.

"You are such a dork," Joyce said.

Gina opened her eyes. "Yes, but I am your dork." Gina sat up. "Helen can't be better than you at everything. Who has the better best friend, huh?" Gina pointed at herself.

Joyce reached out her hand. "I definitely have the better best friend," Joyce said, helping Gina off the ground and then scooting over so that Gina could sit on the sack of rice with her. "You're my best dork."

Gina bumped her shoulder. "Thanks."

"I just don't understand why they hugged," Joyce said, starting to feel miserable again.

"Don't worry about it. I'm sure John just knows Helen from some stupid club."

"But now that he knows where she works, he'll want to see her all the time," Joyce said, kicking the sack with her heel.

"You don't know that, Joyce. Just talk to Helen and ask her about John."

"I don't want to know."

"Yes you do," Gina said.

"Yeah, well, whatever Helen wants, Helen gets," Joyce said.

"Stop being so negative."

"I'm just saying what's true."

"Joyce, you don't know that Helen even likes John. Why would she want to go out with someone in high school? Just because you think he's a total babe does not mean everyone else is panting over him. Look at me," Gina said, pointing at herself. "You see me being a complete fool for that weird light brown hair and lurch walk?"

"His hair is auburn, and he has to walk that way 'cause of all his muscles. Surfing takes at lot of strength, you know."

Gina continued to stare her down.

Joyce sighed. Gina did have a point. John was younger than Helen, and even if he liked her, it didn't mean that Helen liked him. Perhaps not everyone was as impressed as Joyce was with John Ford Kang.

"Okay, you're right." Joyce stood up. "Come on, we should go help out in front."

"It'll be fun working together," Gina said, linking arms. "I got your back."

"Thanks." Joyce smiled.

Before Joyce had a chance to speak with Helen about John, the dinner crowd began to stream in. Gina and Joyce worked quickly, showing customers to their tables and taking their orders before bringing out the small plates of banchan. At the height of the dinner rush, when almost all the tables were taken, Gomo walked into the restaurant with a young man in a blue suit. Joyce almost tripped with her large tray loaded with rice, bulgoki and jap-che when she saw the two of them standing near the door. Apa quickly stashed his book under the counter before getting up to hobble over to the front.

Apa bowed and greeted Gomo and her guest.

"Joyce." Gomo waved.

"One minute, Gomo," Joyce called back as she set the tray down at a table with a family of five and unloaded the food. After making sure the family was all set, Joyce quickly hurried over to Apa, Gomo and her guest.

Joyce bowed and greeted Gomo.

"Joyce, this is Mr. Moon," Gomo said, her face twitching into a smile as she introduced him. "Mr. Moon, this is my youngest niece, Joyce."

"On-young-ha-say-yo," Mr. Moon said and bowed.

When he straightened back up, Joyce noticed that he had a rather square head but pleasant enough features. Joyce wondered why Gomo was dining with him. She usually brought her friends, women her age from church, to the restaurant, not some young guy who looked like he worked at a bank or something.

Joyce bowed back and mumbled her greeting.

Gomo touched Joyce's elbow and whispered, "Where is your sister?"

"In the back with Mrs. Lee," Joyce whispered back. She could see a couple who had been waiting to be seated start to frown in annoyance. "Let me take care of these people first, Gomo, and then I will get Helen for you."

Gomo glanced over her shoulder at the other couple. "Mr. Moon and I are here to eat. We can sit over there," Gomo said and pointed at the last empty table.

Before Joyce and Apa could protest, Gomo led Mr. Moon over to the table. Joyce sighed and shook her head. Apa turned to apologize to the angry twosome, but they were already heading for the door. Joyce headed to the kitchen while Apa limped over to talk to Gomo and take their orders.

Helen and Mrs. Lee were working quickly and efficiently together in the kitchen. There was no mad scrambling or shouting instructions from across the room like there had been when Joyce was working in the back.

"I almost have your order ready," Helen said as she quickly plated some marinated tofu and poured some sauce on top. Helen handed the dish to Joyce.

"Gomo's out there with some Mr. Moon guy," Joyce said, taking the plate.

"Who?" Helen looked confused.

Joyce shrugged. "Mr. Moon. Gomo wants to see you."

Helen took a deep breath. "Can you tell her I'll be out in another half hour or so?"

"Do you want me to handle the back while you go see her right now?" Joyce asked.

"NO!" Helen and Mrs. Lee both said at the same time.

"Fine." Joyce scowled and left with the plate of tofu.

On her way to deliver the order, Joyce stopped by Mr. Moon and Gomo's table to report that Helen would be with them shortly, after the dinner rush had let up a bit. Joyce saw a tiny flicker of anger wrinkle Gomo's nose, which was the only part of Gomo's face that could really move, but Mr. Moon seemed perfectly content to wait. Joyce caught him squinting and studying her face as she spoke to Gomo.

"We need tea and some water," Gomo said right before Joyce turned to leave.

Joyce nodded and rushed to drop off the marinated tofu with an older gentleman dining alone and then she made her way to the wet bar behind the register counter to fill Gomo's drink order. Gina met up with her and picked up another pitcher of water.

"Who is he?" Gina whispered.

"I have no idea," Joyce whispered back, filling two water glasses with ice. "He seems kind of formal, like a banker or something. Maybe he's handling Gomo's big lottery money."

Gina quickly glanced over her shoulder. "Definitely not a banker. More like sales."

Joyce grabbed two teacups and poured some warm barley tea. "How do you know?"

"Look at those shoes," Gina said. "Brown shoes with a blue suit. Please. And the heels are really worn down. Definitely in sales and not at some classy place, either." Gina took off to deliver the water to one of her tables.

Joyce shook her head. Gina should work for the CIA or something. Joyce delivered the tea and water to Gomo and Mr. Moon, who was nodding his head at something Gomo was saying.

"Joyce. Please tell your sister she can at least come out of the kitchen to greet us."

"Yes, Gomo," Joyce said and headed back to the kitchen.

Apa was sitting on his stool at the register, finalizing the tab for one of her tables and glancing over at Gomo and Mr. Moon with a worried expression on his face.

"Helen," Joyce called out from the entrance to the kitchen. "Gomo wants you to come out and at least say hello."

Helen pulled her chopsticks out of a jar of kimchee. Her face began to color as red as the spicy chili seasoning on the cabbage. She set down her chopsticks and followed Joyce out into the dining room. Apa held up a check, and Joyce picked it up to deliver to the family that was ready to leave. Helen headed over to Gomo and Mr. Moon's table.

"Gam-sah-ham-nee-da," Joyce said to the family, presenting the check and picking up their empty plates. As she headed back into the kitchen to deposit the dirty dishes with Juan, she watched as Helen approached the table and Mr. Moon quickly scrambled out of the booth to stand up. Helen began to bow just as Mr. Moon thrust out a small gift-wrapped box, smacking Helen in the forehead.

"Ai! Me-on-heh-yo," Mr. Moon cried and grabbed his glass of ice water.

Helen grimaced in pain and backed away just as Mr. Moon tried to press the cold glass to her forehead. A cascade of water spilled down the front of Helen's apron.

Gomo sat stiffly watching the exchange and then barked, "Sit down, Mr. Moon."

"Please accept my deepest apology," he said gloomily before sitting down.

Gomo leaned forward and grabbed the gift out of his hand.

"For you," Gomo said and handed it to Helen.

Gina raised one eyebrow at Joyce as they passed each other, their laughter barely contained.

As Joyce headed out of the kitchen, Helen was hurrying back inside.

"He's smooth," Joyce said at the doorway.

Helen's face was almost purple with rage. "I don't have time for this," she said gruffly and hurried past.

"Look who's projecting now," Joyce said to Helen's

back. She turned around and caught Apa furtively thumbing through his book, with his back to Gomo and Mr. Moon. Of all the times to be reading, Joyce thought. Apa was really taking this mystery novel a little too seriously.

By the time the dinner rush let up, Gomo and Mr. Moon had finished their meal and were waiting patiently for Helen to join them. Apa stood by their table asking Mr. Moon questions while Gomo fired daggers with her eyes at Apa.

"So, Mr. Moon, do you not agree that women need time to explore their own identity before they settle down?"

Mr. Moon looked confused. "Identity?"

"And in this modern age, do you believe in"—Apa searched for the word—"yes, in fluidity?"

"What?"

Gomo grabbed Joyce's hand as she was passing. "Hurry and get your sister."

"Yes, Gomo," Joyce said and went off to the kitchen to hurry Helen so that she could come and stop Apa from rambling even more. Where was he getting all the weird questions?

"Mrs. Lee," Joyce said, looking around the kitchen. "Where is Helen?"

Mrs. Lee was cleaning the grill and nodded her head at the storage room.

Joyce walked over and stood in the doorway. Helen was sitting on the exact same sack of rice that Joyce had been sitting on earlier in the evening.

"Helen, what are you doing? They've been waiting for you all night," Joyce said.

"I can't go out there," Helen mumbled.

"Why?"

"He's supposed to be my date. He wants to take me to some karaoke place," Helen said miserably.

Joyce started to smile. "Ohhhh. He's from that dating service."

Helen sighed.

"Well, he's not that ugly. He probably wants to serenade you. Just make sure not to stand too close to him, in case he trips or something."

"It doesn't matter what he looks like or what he wants to sing. I don't want to go out with him."

Joyce rolled her eyes. Helen was acting like she had to get a cavity filled. What was so wrong with letting a guy take her out?

"It's just one date," Joyce muttered and started to turn away.

Helen's head sank even farther. "Yeah, right," she

sighed. "First it'll be one date and then he'll start calling and want to have dinner and then he'll want the kiss good night. And then"—Helen pulled out a small jewelry box from the front pocket of her apron—"they all want more."

Joyce had never seen Helen so dejected before. Joyce was the one who usually had problems. Not Helen.

Helen fiddled with the box and stared off into space. "Or they start stalking you. Calling your cell phone and dropping by where you work, like that guy earlier tonight."

Joyce cocked her head. "What guy?"

Helen shrugged and slowly began to open the box. "Some guy from your high school. He was on student council." She pulled out one rose-colored, heart-shaped gemstone earring. "I think he's a junior or senior. Why would I date someone as young as my sister?"

Helen placed the earring back in the box and muttered, "It's like an arranged marriage or something."

"What's his name?" Joyce croaked and stepped into the storage room. Her heart was racing like she had just finished climbing the last hill before riding down to her school.

"John."

"John Ford Kang?"

Helen met Joyce's eyes. "Who else? There's only a handful of Asians in your school."

Joyce strangled back a cry. "He's a Twinkie. A banana. Why would he want to go out with you? He only dates blondes!" Joyce wailed and grabbed on to one of the shelves for support.

Helen stepped back in surprise. "Calm down, Joyce. Not that I want to date him, but he's not that bad. I mean, he is kind of player, but he was always really sweet with me. He said he wanted to hang out more with Korean friends. Have you ever talked to him?"

"Shut up! Just shut up!" Joyce yelled and turned her back to Helen. Joyce wanted to throw something. She wanted to tear up the storage room and rage against the injustice of it all. Why was Helen always the one everyone wanted? Why wasn't Joyce ever good enough? Joyce bowed her head and bit down on her lower lip to keep from crying. She was not going to let Helen see her cry.

"Are you okay?" Helen asked, her hand tentatively patting Joyce's back.

"Don't touch me," Joyce mumbled and jerked away from Helen's touch.

Helen stood still. "Joyce, tell me what's going on."

"Leave me alone!" Joyce yelled.

"Girls!"

Helen and Joyce both turned to the doorway. Gomo stood just inside the storage room, firmly clutching her purse with both hands to her stomach as though to shield herself from any muggers that might be lurking in the back kitchen.

"What is all this yelling?" Gomo asked. "Helen, Mr. Moon and I have been waiting for you all night. Do not embarrass me in front of our guest."

Helen bowed her head.

"He has been very patient." Gomo beckoned Helen.

Helen walked over to Gomo.

"I'm sorry, Gomo," Helen said softly.

Gomo stared at Helen's sorrowful face. She smoothed Helen's hair back and took in Helen's oil-splattered apron. "Are you worried about how you look?" Gomo asked. "I have my purse. You may use my makeup if you would like, but you do not need anything. Just change out of your apron. Now, where are the earrings?"

Helen fished inside her pocket and pulled out the small jewelry box.

"Put them on," Gomo said, smiling. "He will be so pleased to see you wearing his gift."

Helen carefully took the earrings out of the box

and placed them in her unadorned earlobes. The small heart-shaped jewels perfectly matched the rose blush of Helen's cheeks.

Gomo beamed with pride as though she had picked them out herself, which Joyce would not have put past her.

"Do not be nervous, Helen. Just be yourself and he will see what a wonderful person you are. Truly beautiful inside and out." Gomo draped her arm around Helen's shoulder and shepherded her out of the storage area.

As Helen began to round the corner of the doorway, she glanced back at Joyce. And for a moment, in that last heartbreaking look, Joyce couldn't tell who was more unhappy, Helen or herself.

Joyce followed them out of the storage room. Helen's back was hunched forward, her feet barely shuffling along. As angry as Joyce was at Helen, she couldn't help but feel sorry for her, too. Gomo pulled on Helen's arm to make her walk faster. For once, Joyce was relieved not to be the perfect older sister.

TWELVE

joyce woke up the next morning and walked out into the living room to find most of her family laid up as though she had entered a hospital. And even though it was a Sunday and they should have been getting ready for church, the television was turned on to the Korean channel. Uhmma and Apa sat on opposite ends of the couch. Uhmma was watching television and cradling Apa's swollen black-and-blue ankle on her lap, while Apa sat on the other side intently reading his mystery novel. Andy sat on a large folded beach towel in the armchair.

Uhmma looked up as Joyce approached. Her forehead was slightly smaller, the skin showing some wrinkles instead of being taut as a balloon. Joyce leaned over the back of the couch and gave Uhmma a peck on the cheek.

"Are you feeling better?" Joyce asked.

Uhmma nodded, tiny points of light coming from her now visible eyes. She gingerly poked her forehead. "The swelling is going down."

Joyce studied Uhmma's eyebrows, which had begun to look slightly off center and crooked now that the swelling had receded. Joyce didn't want to say anything to make Uhmma more upset. Apa looked up from his book and offered his cheek for a kiss.

"Good morning, Apa," Joyce said and gave him a peck as well. "Did you find out who did it yet? Your ankle looks better."

"It does not feel better," Apa sighed. "I might have to go to the hospital, after all. I will give it one more day of rest."

Joyce nodded and glanced over at Andy, who was zoning out on the Korean soap opera. "How ya doing, poopy?"

Andy scowled. "Shut up."

"Joyce, please tell your brother to stop taking the shark liver pills," Uhmma urged.

"You're still taking them after all that moaning last night about how Gomo poisoned you?" Joyce asked and walked over to the kitchen to get herself a bowl of cereal.

Andy perked up. "I called Tom this morning to ask if anything unusual had happened to him when he started taking the pills."

"I can't believe Tom Koh would admit that he had the runs," Joyce said, pouring cereal into a bowl.

"Well, he wouldn't exactly admit to anything, but he did say that whatever it was, it would pass," Andy said.

"So you two had an entire conversation about diarrhea without naming it?" Joyce poured milk over her cereal. She stared down into her bowl. "Why am I having this conversation before breakfast?"

Andy turned back to the show. "It's not diarrhea. It's a side effect. And it should stop after my body gets used to the pills."

Uhmma shook her head. "The pills are too strong for you."

"I just want to try them for another week," Andy pleaded.

The phone rang. Joyce picked it up.

"You'll never guess who had the eyelid surgery," Gina said.

Joyce took a bite of her cereal. "How did you know it was me?" she crunched into the phone.

"Well, everyone in your family is injured, and Helen picked up my mom for the early church service, so that just leaves you."

Joyce was impressed. She took another bite of cereal before she realized that, once again, she was carless. Helen had been the good girl, waking up early to fill in for Uhmma. Usually, Uhmma and Mrs. Lee went to the early morning service so that they could help prepare the food to set out for fellowship after the regular service.

"So are you going to guess?"

Joyce crunched some more. "Uhm, I don't know, Lisa Yim."

"WHAT! How did you know?"

Joyce dropped her spoon. "Really! Lisa Yim had the fold done?"

"You could have at least pretended you didn't know," Gina said, her voice deep with disappointment.

"Honestly, I was just guessing!" Joyce fiddled with her spoon. Lisa Yim was one of the pretty college girls that had started going to their church this fall. She and Helen attended the same university, but they never socialized. Lisa tended to hang out with a more sophisticated group. She was originally from New York City, which gave her an air of authority and made her instantly hip.

"Wow! I had no idea. I mean, she came to church with her eyes already creased and everything. I just thought they were natural, like Sharon Kim's. Remember, there was that one time Lisa's boobs grew, like, two bra sizes, and we talked about how she must have had some work done, but that was just a joke. That was a joke, right?"

Gina sighed. "I don't know about her boobs, but she definitely got the folds."

"How do you know for sure?"

Gina started to get excited again as she retraced the Korean grapevine she had tapped for the information. She went through about six unfamiliar names before she got to one that Joyce recognized. "Mrs. Shin."

Joyce gasped. "Mrs. Shin never talks smack!"

"I know!" Gina squealed back. "That's how I know this is one hundred percent true."

"Wow," Joyce said again and leaned over her bowl of cereal.

"So, we'll ask her about the surgery at church today and you can get firsthand information."

"Whoa, wait a minute," Joyce said, standing up straight. "I can't just go up to Lisa Yim and ask her about her eyelid surgery."

"Why not?"

"That's just weird."

"Don't you want to know?"

"Well, yeah. But."

"But what? Just ask her."

"It seems too personal."

"Oh, please. We live in Los Angeles County, how personal can plastic surgery be?"

"You have a point."

"I'll pick you up for church in half an hour."

"Okay. Bye."

Joyce put down the phone and resumed eating her now soggy cereal. Lisa Yim. Wow. She was so pretty. And confident. She was always making announcements about some Bible study group or after-church volley-ball game.

"Lisa Yim is a babe," Andy called out.

Joyce gave up trying to eat her cereal and put her bowl in the sink.

"Stop eavesdropping, Andy," Joyce said as she walked back to her room to change for church.

"Stop talking so loud," Andy called after her.

⬯

Joyce and Gina stood outside on the lawn after church service was over. A row of bushes separated them from the cement courtyard outside of the fellowship hall. Joyce and Gina tried to look nonchalant as they spied through the leaves and branches at Lisa Yim and her entourage of college men. When she wasn't the one talking, widening and narrowing her eyes with drama, Lisa sipped her coffee and listened, smiling provocatively, her head tilted just so in a gesture of extreme interest.

Joyce stared over Gina's shoulder and licked her chocolate-glazed doughnut while making a mental note to practice smiling like Lisa in the mirror when she got home.

"I don't think I can go through with this," Joyce said to Gina.

"Oh, come on, Joyce. How else are you going to find out what the surgery is like?"

"I already looked it up on the Internet. It's not pretty, Gina. I couldn't even read the information without holding up my hand to block out the surgery photos."

"Really?" Gina said. "Gross."

"Exactly." Joyce took a bite of her doughnut. "I'm not sure if I even want the surgery," she mumbled.

Gina cut her eyes back to Joyce. "What are you saying?"

"I'm saying what's the point? John already likes Helen. And besides, it's not like the folds are going to make me gorgeous or something. How are two little lines above my eyes going to make John Ford Kang suddenly see me or make me more confident? I'm such a loser, I couldn't even go out there and say hello to him." Joyce licked the chocolate off the doughnut. "Besides, what if I have a reaction to some chemical like my mom?"

Gina reached over and grabbed the doughnut out of Joyce's hand and threw it into the bushes. She held Joyce's shoulders and stared hard into her eyes. "Joyce, I say this as your friend. What about 'free' don't you get? You can't just throw this opportunity away!"

"But you just threw away my doughnut."

Gina held up her hand. "Stop with the chocolate."

Joyce scowled.

Gina took a deep breath. "Joyce, you're not going to some nasty Korean tattoo parlor—she's going to take you to a reputable plastic surgeon. Think about how great you felt after the makeover. It'll be like that, only permanent. And if nothing else, would you at least do it for me so that I can live vicariously through you? God, I need some excitement in my life."

Joyce stared at the half-eaten doughnut partially hidden by the leaves.

"If I had an aunt like that, I would be kissing her butt."

Joyce stopped staring at her doughnut and searched for Gomo, finding her sitting with some older ladies in a circle at the far end of the courtyard. If Uhmma had been around serving doughnuts, coffee and Korean vegetable tempura like she usually did, Joyce would have already been over to give Gomo the obligatory kiss on the cheek while all the other ladies cooed and said how lucky Gomo was to have such cha-keh, thoughtful nieces.

"Look around you, Joyce. Look at Mr. Shin," Gina pointed out. Joyce stared over at the wrinkled old man holding his cane and smiling widely at one of his grandchildren.

"What if he decided not to get those dentures? You think he would be smiling so hard? Or So Young Choi. What if she never got the laser eye surgery and still wore those ugly glasses? Do you think she would be dating David Kim right now? And little Christina Chang. What if her uhmma and apa let her keep her original ears?" Gina asked, her fingers pulling out her ears in a ninety-degree angle from her head.

"What are you saying?" Joyce asked, her eyes wandering from person to person, making a mental checklist of what had changed and what needed to change. Christina Chang never knew what it was like to have satellite ears, but anyone who had seen her as a baby remembered. There was Bobby Song walking to his car, he had a mole on his cheek so large it made it hard to talk to him without starting to count the hairs growing out of it. And Mrs. Yoo, she had just come over from rural Korea, and her teeth showed it.

"We all do things to look better. Everyone, even the most perfect-looking person, could use a tweak here and there," Gina said.

Joyce spotted Helen walking over to Gomo. All the older ladies around Gomo broke out into grins and began to chatter wildly to Helen. Gomo raised her cheek for Helen's kiss and then held Helen's hand as Gomo spoke to her friends. Helen stared off into the distance while the other ladies began to lean forward in excitement and wave their hands in the air. Gomo was probably bragging about how Helen had embarked on the dating odyssey.

"Oh, no! Where did she go?" Gina said.

Joyce's eyes swiveled over to the group they had been observing. The men were still there, but Lisa had disappeared. Gina was craning her neck trying to see better over the bushes.

"I don't see her," Joyce said.

Gina grabbed her hand. "Come on."

The two of them searched everywhere, inside the church, in the kitchen, over at the office. Joyce quickly crouched behind a wooden bench when she saw Gomo looking in her direction. Gina spotted Sam at the far end of the lawn area taking pictures and ran over to him. Joyce stayed crouched down. She wanted to make sure the coast was clear before she ran across such an exposed area. Joyce slowly raised her head and peeked over at the spot where she last saw Gomo. The chair was empty. Joyce sprang up to make a mad dash over to Sam and Gina.

"Joyce!" Gomo barked.

"Ahhh!" Joyce fell back to the ground in fear and surprise. Gomo loomed over her. Gomo's shark eyes bore holes into Joyce's face.

"Hi, Gomo," Joyce said, waving.

"What kind of ladylike behavior is this?" Gomo lectured. "Why are you and Gina sneaking around the church?"

"We're just looking for someone, Gomo," Joyce said. She stood up and brushed off her slacks.

"You two look like crazy girls. Sit down and stop being so foolish."

Joyce sighed. "Yes, Gomo."

"How is your uhmma?"

"She's a little better."

Gomo clutched her purse. "Those people made a big mistake treating your uhmma that way. Why they did not ask the proper questions, I do not understand. I spoke with them and they will refund all the money, but they refuse to pay for your uhmma's doctor expenses. They said that she signed a release form. Those people have no dignity. Tell your uhmma I will take care of it."

"Yes, Gomo."

Gomo turned to leave and then turned back around. "And your appointment with Dr. Rie-ne-or is Tuesday. I will pick you up in the morning."

"What?" Joyce said. "I can't do the surgery Tuesday. I'm not ready!"

Gomo harrumphed. "Aigoo, Joyce. This is a consultation to see what shape of fold will look the best. Be a good girl and do not embarrass me."

Gomo turned and walked away.

"Joyce," Gina called out, waving her over.

She ran to her friends.

"Hey, Sam," Joyce said breathlessly.

"What did your Gomo want?" Gina asked.

"I have to go for a consultation with her on Tuesday," Joyce said and raised one eyebrow at Gina as she cut her eyes to Sam so that Gina wouldn't ask any more questions in front of him. Joyce changed the subject.

"Hey, Sam, have you seen Lisa Yim anywhere?" she asked.

"I just asked him that," Gina said.

Sam snapped a few pictures of Joyce.

She bowed her head so that he couldn't get a clear shot of her face.

"Joyce, you promised," Sam said from behind the camera. "I need some head shots."

"Head what?" Gina asked.

Joyce looked up. "I told Sam he could take pictures of my face if he helped at the restaurant last night."

"Joyce is going to model for a project that I'm doing," Sam said as a whirr of clicks went off.

Gina put one hand on her hip. "What's wrong with my face?"

Sam grinned. "I'll get your face next."

"Can you Photoshop them so my cheeks don't look so squirrelly?" Gina asked.

"I work with real film, Gina," Sam said as he clicked off a few more shots.

Gina scowled. "Maybe I won't pose for you, then. At least not until my cheeks are a little thinner."

Sam finally put down his camera. "What were you two asking me?"

"Lisa Yim," Gina said. "Have you seen her?"

Sam thought for a second. "Is she the one with long black hair?"

Gina made a strangling noise at the back of her throat. Joyce bit her lower lip to keep from laughing. Sam caught Joyce's eyes and the two of them burst.

"Very funny," Gina said. "You would think after centuries that Asian women would try and style their hair differently."

Joyce reached out and touched Gina's long black hair. "It's the only thing we have for anyone to covet," Joyce said.

Sam waved his camera in the direction of the bathroom. "If she's the one I think you two are thinking of, I saw her head toward the bathroom right before you two found me."

Gina and Joyce took off running for the bathroom.

Sam called out after them, "Hey, what about my photos!"

Gina skidded to a stop before the closed bathroom door. The church had once been an old Catholic school, and the bathroom still had a line of toilet stalls on one side of the room with a line of sinks on the opposite side. Gina put her finger to her lips before carefully pushing open the swinging door. They tiptoed inside.

The doors to the toilet stalls were all open except one. Gina motioned for Joyce to follow her into the nearest stall. Joyce tried to be silent and stealthy like Gina but ended up sounding like a clunking horse. Gina and Joyce crammed into the stall together and closed the door. The crashing sound of a toilet flushing made them both freeze. A high-pitched squeak followed next as someone exited the stall.

Gina whispered in Joyce's ear, "I'm going to stand on top of the toilet."

Joyce gave her a puzzled look.

"So she won't see both our feet," Gina whispered and carefully climbed onto the toilet and crouched down. Joyce shook her head. Gina always managed to amaze her with her plans.

Joyce pressed her eyes to the narrow band of space between the stall door and the divider for the next stall. Lisa Yim was walking over to the sink in her black high heels and clinging, knee-length black silk dress. Her long straight hair swung gently from side to side. She set her purse down on the counter and turned on the water to wash her hands.

Joyce turned around and gave Gina the thumbs-up about finding Lisa. Slowly, Joyce unlocked the stall door and slipped out, making sure the door did not swing wide open. Behind her, the toilet flushed magically. Joyce jumped. Lisa glanced up to the mirror and caught Joyce's eyes in the reflection. A maniacal grin leaped to Joyce's face as she quickly made her way over to the sinks. Lisa smiled back and resumed looking in her purse.

Lisa pulled out her lipstick and leaned toward the mirror. Joyce stood two sinks down from her and turned on the water. She purposefully stared down at her hands, but in her peripheral vision she could see

Lisa carefully pressing her lips together after reapplying her lipstick and then quickly running her index finger under her eyes to remove any mascara smudges. Joyce kept lathering her hands with soap. Lisa glanced over at Joyce before dropping her lipstick back into her purse and closing it with a snap. Lisa stepped back and checked her reflection one last time.

Joyce's heart thudded. This was it. Lisa was about to leave. Gina was going to kill her if Joyce blew this chance.

As Lisa turned to walk out, Joyce stepped back and blocked Lisa's path. Lisa paused midstep. Joyce's wet hands dripped water on the floor.

"Excuse me," Lisa said and stepped out of the way.

Joyce frantically shook the water from her hands. "Uhm, Lisa, right?"

Lisa tilted her head to one side. "Yes?"

Joyce shook her hands some more. "I have a question."

Lisa nodded.

Joyce blurted out, "This is kind of weird and personal and I don't want to invade your privacy or anything. But I don't know anyone else to ask and my aunt is taking me in for a consultation Tuesday and I want to get as much information as possible so we, I mean, I followed you in here. Not that I'm trying to stalk you or anything, but I hope you don't mind."

Lisa frowned. "Was that your question?"

"What question?"

"That I don't mind?"

"Huh? Mind what?"

Lisa took a deep breath. "Just stop talking for a second. I feel like we're playing who's on first."

"Who's on first?" Joyce asked, nervously shaking out her wet hands again.

Lisa walked over to the paper towel dispenser and pulled out some sheets. She walked back and handed them to Joyce.

"Thanks," Joyce said gratefully.

"Let's start over, okay?" Lisa said. "What's your name?"

"Joyce. Joyce Park."

"Oh," Lisa said, a look of recognition brightening her eyes. "Are you Helen's sister?"

Joyce nodded and dried her hands on the paper towels.

"Helen and I don't really know each other too well, even though we go to the same college, but I've heard a lot about your family from my cousin Su Yon," Lisa said.

"Oh." Joyce nodded. "I didn't know Su Yon had any relatives in Los Angeles."

"Well, Su Yon isn't exactly a blood relative. Her mother and my mother grew up in the same village in Korea."

"So funny how everyone is connected," Joyce said. "We miss Su Yon. How is she doing?"

Lisa shrugged. "It's been a while since I've spoken to her. Last I heard, she and her mother had moved."

Joyce nodded, scrunching up the paper towels in her hands. If Lisa knew Su Yon, then she had to be nice. Joyce started to feel more comfortable about asking Lisa to talk about the eyelid surgery. "Uhm, so, Lisa, I have this really personal question."

"No problem. What did you want to know?"

Joyce worried the paper towels. "It's about the fold. You know, the eyelid surgery."

Lisa held out her hand for the paper towels. Joyce handed them over.

"So you want to get your eyelids done?" Lisa asked and walked over to the trash.

Joyce leaned back against the sink counter. "Yes. No." Joyce slumped. "I don't know."

Lisa threw away the paper towels and walked back over to Joyce. Lisa stood in front of the mirror with perfect posture, her shoulders thrown back, the thin black silk clinging to her breasts, accentuating all the curves. "Do you want to look at my eyes?"

Joyce stared at her chest. "Your eyes?"

"My eyes. Look." Lisa turned and leaned toward Joyce. "I had them done in high school for my sixteenth birthday."

Joyce gazed at Lisa's eyes, focusing on the twin crescent creases lined in kohl.

"It's not that big a surgery," Lisa said. She blinked a few times so that Joyce could see the full effect. Lisa leaned back.

"I think it took a couple of weeks to fully heal, and there's a lot of pain at first, not to mention that you have to sleep semi-sitting up, but the end results are fabulous."

"Wow," Joyce said quietly.

Lisa studied Joyce's face. "You don't seem wowed."

Joyce sighed. "Do you really think it makes that big a difference in how you look? I mean, you're so pretty anyway, it's not like you needed the surgery to make yourself look better."

Lisa thought for a second. "Honestly, it's not so

much the way you look but the way you feel." Lisa stepped to the side and stared at herself in the mirror. "When I was in New York, I went to this really exclusive prep school. I wasn't exactly teased, but I wasn't getting a ton of offers for dates, either. There were plenty of Asians at my school, and the ones who were getting noticed definitely looked a certain way."

Joyce perked up. "Yeah, I know exactly what you mean."

Lisa peeled her eyes away from her own reflection and met Joyce's eyes. "After the surgery, I just felt more confident. My eyes looked fuller and more defined. And for the first time in my life, I could actually wear eye shadow without it looking weird! I started dressing better and talking more to people. And I finally had the confidence to start flirting with this really cute boy that I had been crushing on since ninth grade, and he asked me out. It was amazing how different I felt after the surgery."

Joyce nodded in a trance. "All from just two creases on your eyelids."

Lisa smiled. "Getting the fold changed my life."

"WOW!"

Lisa flipped her long black hair over her shoulder. "You know, people have this hang-up about plastic surgery. Like it's not natural or something. If it's God's will to make you look a certain way, it's also God's will that he created doctors who can help you improve your looks. And ultimately, if it makes you feel better, then what's wrong with that?"

"Yeah," Joyce said.

"I have to get going," Lisa said. "Are you going to volleyball practice Tuesday afternoon?"

Joyce shook her head. "I don't play."

"You don't have to play. Just come watch and hang out. A bunch of us are going to be there. We can talk more then, if you have other questions. Anyway, we'll be at the far end of the boardwalk at the beach."

"Uhm, okay," Joyce said.

Lisa turned to the side to leave, her buxom figure coming into profile.

"Hey, Lisa?" Joyce said.

Lisa turned back.

"Did you do a little something-something to your, you know." Joyce waved her hands near the vicinity of her chest.

One corner of Lisa's lips turned up mysteriously. "What do you think?"

Her high heels clicked tiny precise beats as Lisa left the bathroom.

Gina lunged out of the toilet stall and started shaking out her legs. "Oh, man, these calf cramps are killing me. I thought she was never going to leave."

Joyce stared at herself in the mirror. She wanted to feel different. She wanted guys to gather around her. She wanted to wear silk dresses and high heels. She wanted John Ford Kang and the confidence to go after him.

"I want to be a part of the fold," Joyce said.

joycey-ya," Uhmma whispered, gently shaking Joyce's shoulders.

Joyce barely parted her lids. Gray early morning light filtered into the room.

Uhmma shook her again. "You must get ready for Gomo."

"Huh?" Joyce said, closing her eyes.

Uhmma shook her again. "Joyce. Wake up."

Joyce yawned and opened her eyes. Across the room, Helen's huddled body lay sleeping. Uhmma stood above her, making sure Joyce was really awake this time.

"You must shower and get ready. Gomo will be here in an hour. Make sure you wear clean underwear,"

Uhmma said. Her face was almost back to normal, except for a slight bulgy spot under her new eyebrows.

Joyce stretched her arms up into the air. "What time is it?"

Uhmma turned to go. "Almost seven o'clock."

"Why is Gomo coming so early?" Joyce asked.

"The appointment is at nine o'clock. You know how Gomo hates to be late." Uhmma pulled back the covers. "Sit up."

Joyce swung her legs out of bed and sat up, pulling the covers over her shoulders. She slouched and yawned again. "Why do I have to shower and wear clean underwear if he's looking at my eyes? I could sleep for another hour," Joyce argued.

Uhmma made a clucking noise with her tongue as she left the room, letting Joyce know there was no room for protesting. Joyce pushed herself out of bed.

"Uhmma!" Joyce called out. "Can I have the day off today? The church is having this volleyball game at the beach this afternoon."

Uhmma poked her head back in the room. "Ask your sister if she can cover for you."

After her shower, Joyce started to feel the excitement of what was about to happen. She was on her way to getting the folds. Her entire life was about to change.

As Joyce stood in front of the closet trying to decide what to wear, Helen stirred from her sleep.

"What are you doing up so early?" Helen yawned.

Joyce pulled out a short red jersey tank dress. "Gomo is taking me for my initial consultation with Dr. Reiner."

Helen sat up in bed. "You're seriously thinking of going through with the surgery?"

Joyce put the dress back in. Too short. As much as she had loved it when she bought it, she could never stop thinking about how her legs looked whenever she wore it, which was only once after Andy teased her relentlessly about the fat pockets above her knees.

"Joyce!"

"What?" Joyce said, scanning the closet again. She flipped through all her outfits.

"Why are you going to defile your face like that?"

"What are you talking about, Helen?" Joyce said, feeling frustrated with her inability to choose an outfit. Joyce turned around and walked to her dresser, ready to pull out her default jeans and T-shirt.

Helen got out of bed. "It's ridiculous that you are conforming to these Western standards of beauty. Our eyes are supposed to be like this," she said and pointed to her creaseless upper lids.

Joyce pulled out her jeans. "That's easy for you to say, Helen, because your eyes are huge, and you don't have a problem with them, but you can't just go around shooting your psychobabble mouth off about Western beauty. It's not like I hate my Asian eyes, I just want them to be fuller. More defined."

"Joyce, this isn't like getting fake eyelashes or stick-on nails or something. This is permanent. Do you know what the risks are for this procedure? Have you even taken the time to research what it's all about?"

"Yes, Helen. As a matter of fact, I have taken the time to research the surgery." Joyce pulled on her T-shirt. "So why don't you worry about dating Mr. Moon instead of what I'm going to look like."

Helen slumped back onto her bed.

"Are you going to be around this morning?" Joyce asked.

"Yeah, why?" Helen was staring dejectedly out the window.

"I'm going to need the car."

"Well, I have this meeting."

"You always have a meeting. I just want to use the car once this summer."

Uhmma called from the living room, "Joyce, Gomo is here!"

Joyce quickly grabbed a pair of socks on her way out.

"We can talk about it when you get back," Helen said and got back into bed.

Gomo drove so slowly down the freeway, even the cars in the far right lane were passing her by. Joyce tried not to feel embarrassed by all the honking. Joyce shifted in her seat and a loud groaning noise not unlike the sound of a fart escaped from the plastic-covered seats. In fact, the entire car, from the seats to the doors to even the gear shift column, was encased in a protective vinyl covering. Two small wooden Korean masks hung off a tasseled rope from the rear-view mirror. In the backseat, Gomo's small electronic dog lay slumbering.

When Gomo had first gotten the "pet" from Japan, she carried it with her everywhere, bragging that this pet didn't shed or eat disgusting dog food. After the first one got stolen in a mugging, which Gomo insisted had been instigated by her amazing pet, Gomo got another one but kept it hidden away.

"These crazy L.A. drivers," Gomo muttered under her breath as another car passed them, honking loudly.

Joyce thought, So this is why it's going to take an

hour to get downtown. Gomo glanced over at Joyce slouching low in her seat.

"Sit up straight," Gomo ordered.

Joyce sat up.

"Dr. Rie-ne-or is a very busy man. Do not trouble him with too many questions."

Joyce stared out her window. "Yes, Gomo." She thought for a moment about asking Gomo if this was the same doctor who had messed up her nose, but the possibility of opening that can of worms in a slow-moving, closed car was unbearable. Instead she asked, "Will the surgery hurt?"

"Of course," Gomo snapped.

Joyce slumped back into her seat.

Gomo softened her tone. "Do not worry. Dr. Rie-ne-or is the best. Not like those other Korean doctors who were not educated here in the United States. They only know the old procedures. Dr. Rie-ne-or is very smart and he always uses the best equipment." After a moment she added, "He was the one who saved my nose."

Joyce sat up and tried to sneak a peek a Gomo. Her vulture neck was stretched out as far as it would go as she craned her head to see over the dashboard. Her roman profile nose was hardly scarred, even though it had been worked on extensively. Gomo still bragged that her nose was the exact replica of a famous French actress. Maybe Gomo was right. If he could make Michael happy, he had to be good.

"Mi-, I mean, Gomo. Did Dr. Reiner suggest what you should do with your face, or did you go to him because you knew what you wanted to change about yourself?"

Gomo did not answer. Joyce started to get nervous, wondering if she had somehow offended Michael. "What I mean is, does Dr. Reiner do whatever he wants to do, like an artist or something?"

Gomo squinted as the freeway turned toward the east and the early morning sun rose directly in front of them. "I know what you and Andy call me," she said quietly.

Joyce wasn't sure if she had heard correctly. "What did you say, Gomo?" she asked. Joyce wished she could turn on the radio, but Gomo hated to be distracted when she was driving.

"Michael. Like the strange black singer who is not black anymore. He looks like a monster now."

Joyce began to panic. Uhmma was going to kill her. This was terrible. Joyce tried to do damage control.

"No, Gomo. Andy just likes to joke around," Joyce said.

"You think I'm a monster?"

Joyce stared quietly at her hands folded in her lap. Oh, no. Maybe this had been Gomo's plan all along. She was going to take Joyce in, and Dr. Reiner was going to make her look like a monster as payback for all the teasing that Joyce and Andy did behind Gomo's back. Or at least they had thought it was behind her back.

"I hear you and Andy whispering all the time. Michael this. Michael that. I did not understand until I saw a news show about the singer."

Joyce slouched back, the plastic-covered seat moaning as miserably as Joyce felt. She covered her red face with her hands, unable to face Gomo.

Gomo put on her blinker, and the rhythmic clicking sound filled the silent car. Joyce peeked to see that the exit was still a mile away. The blinker tapped out the empty minutes as Joyce thought about what to say.

"It was just a joke," Joyce said weakly and lowered her hands.

"I am not a joke, Joyce."

Joyce nodded, her head bowed in shame and embarrassment.

Gomo sat up straight. "Before I came to the United States with your first uncle Joseph, I was the most beautiful girl in my village. Every day someone would comment about my face. And when your uncle Joseph first saw me, he rewarded our entire family with food from the army just so he could meet me." Gomo glanced quickly over to Joyce to make sure she was paying attention. "Do you know what a great gift that was during a time of war? He fed our whole family for one year."

"Wow," Joyce said. "I didn't know that, Gomo."

Gomo slowly braked and turned the car onto the exit ramp. "Joseph only wanted to talk to me every time he had a break. We fell in love."

Joyce nodded. She knew that part of the history.

Gomo stopped at a red light. She turned sideways and looked directly into Joyce's eyes. "When Joseph finally brought me to the United States, do you know what his family said to me?"

Joyce raised her hand to her face and gnawed at the webbing between her thumb and index finger. Gomo reached over and slapped Joyce's hand away from her face.

"They told him how ugly I was. How could he fall in love with some slanted-eye gook? They would not even talk to me."

Joyce stiffened with anger. It was one thing for Joyce and Andy to tease their aunt, but the thought of someone else insulting Gomo was enough to make Joyce yell, "Assholes! Why didn't you just leave them, Gomo?"

Gomo turned back to the light. "How can a wife leave her husband? Joseph loved me. It was only his family that did not accept who I was," she said with resignation.

"So you changed how you looked so that you could fit in?"

Gomo pushed slowly on the accelerator when the light turned green. "I did not do it for them. I did it for myself. Here, in the United States, everyone wants to look more American. Even the Americans want to look more American. Why do you think there are so many women who diet, change their hair color and make their noses smaller and their chests bigger?"

Gomo flipped on her blinker and slowly took a right turn. A dark brown medical building loomed ahead of them. Gomo lifted up her bony hand and pointed. "In America, everyone is always chasing their dream. I only wanted what I had lost when I moved to this country. I only wanted to be beautiful again."

Gomo parked in the underground parking lot. Before getting out the car, Gomo turned around to coo at Kiki and then threw a towel over her pet. Joyce tried not to meet Gomo's eyes directly now that she knew Gomo's story. All those times that she and Andy laughed and imitated Gomo. Her guilt-ridden conscience silenced all the questions that rose up inside her as they rode the elevator to Dr. Reiner's office.

The nurse quickly checked them in and gave Joyce a questionnaire to fill out. Gomo and Joyce took a seat in the black leather chairs that surrounded a large antique coffee table. Subdued lighting and art on the walls made the space feel like someone's living room rather than a doctor's office. Joyce carefully went through the checklist of diseases that she or a family member might have had or did have. In a section that asked if she had any known allergies, Joyce carefully wrote down that her mother had an allergy to tattoo ink. Gomo thumbed through a magazine while Joyce finished filling out the sheet.

"Joyce." An older woman wearing a white nurse's uniform stood at a door that led down another hallway.

Joyce quickly stood up. Gomo followed. The nurse held up her hand and addressed Gomo. "You can wait here, Mrs. Jones. The doctor will come out to see you after he is done with Joyce."

Gomo looked confused but nodded at the authority in the nurse's voice and sat back down. Joyce clutched the clipboard to her chest and followed the nurse into the hallway.

"Right this way," the nurse said and took Joyce's clipboard before leading her down the hall to an examining room. "I'm just going to take your height and weight and then your blood pressure."

"Should I take my shoes off?" Joyce asked before stepping on the scale.

"Only if you want to," the nurse said.

Joyce thought for a second and then stepped on the scale with her shoes on. The nurse checked Joyce's weight and then filled out a form. Next she had Joyce stand against a wall for her height. Finally, Joyce was allowed to sit while the nurse took her blood pressure. Joyce tried not to stare at the nurse's face, wondering if everyone in the office got work done for free. Maybe it was like the deal that Gina got at the department store. Joyce marveled at the thought of getting plastic surgery at an employee discount of twenty percent off.

"Time to take the picture," the nurse said, taking the stethoscope out of her ears.

"Do I need to change?" Joyce asked.

"No, just stay right where you are," the nurse said and pulled out a digital camera from a cabinet. She aimed it at Joyce's face and snapped. A quick flash went off, blinding Joyce. When her vision cleared, the nurse was standing over a laptop computer set up on a small table with wheels. Joyce tried to peer around the nurse, but she finished too quickly.

"The doctor should be right with you."

"Okay," Joyce said nervously.

The nurse smiled and then closed the door behind her as she left.

Joyce looked around the office. On one wall, there was a poster-sized diagram of all the parts of a face. Blue android eyes stared back at Joyce. On the counter next to the sink, there were the usual glass containers of tongue depressants and cotton balls, next to a box of Kleenex and rubber gloves. Except for the computer, it was not so different from her pediatrician's office.

There was a knock at the door. "May I come in?"

"Yes," Joyce said.

A heavily bearded man in his late fifties entered the room. He held a clipboard in one hand and stretched out his right hand for a handshake.

"Hi, Joyce, I'm Dr. Reiner," he said and had a seat in the opposite swiveling chair. "Nice to meet a family member of one of our favorite clients."

"Hi," Joyce said shyly and shook his hand.

Dr. Reiner leaned over and set his clipboard down

on the counter. He sat back in his chair and crossed one leg over the other. "So, Joyce," he said, "what brings you to my office?"

"Uhm, oh, I thought my aunt had already spoken with you." Joyce pointed at her eyes. "The eyelid surgery."

Dr. Reiner nodded. "Yes, your aunt did express her desire for you to undergo blepharoplasty."

Joyce tried to say that silently in her head. She was too nervous to ask him to repeat it.

"However, what your aunt wants and what you want might be two separate things."

Joyce nodded. "Well, I think I would like to get the folds."

Dr. Reiner swiveled around and reached for his clipboard. He flipped through a few pages before handing the clipboard over to Joyce. There was a series of before and after photos of Asian eyes that had undergone the surgery. Dr. Reiner pushed off from the floor and he and his chair rolled over to the large poster of the face. He pointed to the upper eyelid on the face.

"Let me go over the procedure and then we can talk about the complications and risks involved."

Joyce cringed at the words *risks* and *complications*.

"There are a number of ways to achieve a more defined pretarsal crease. While Asian eyes do have folds, the muscle is just attached to the eyelid at such a low point, it is hard to see it. Your eyes are not going to be necessarily bigger with the surgery," he said, widening his eyes as far as possible. "But what we will do is reattach the muscle higher so the pretarsal crease will be more substantial and give a fuller, possibly rounder, look to the eyes."

Joyce nodded.

"Now, since you are a teenager, there are certain considerations that you must take into account." He paused for a second, studying the poster before pushing himself off and rolling over to where Joyce was sitting. "You are still growing," he said with serious concern narrowing his eyes. He pointed to his head and then his heart. "Mentally, emotionally, not to mention that your face and body might still be changing."

Joyce blushed and prayed that he wouldn't ask when she started her period.

Dr. Reiner thoughtfully held his bearded chin. "Many teenagers come to my office with requests for breast augmentation and liposuction and blepharoplasty. And when I see these young adults, I wonder if nothing but a good dose of self-confidence, exercise and a lesson at the makeup counter might not be all they really need. Do you understand what I'm saying, Joyce?"

Joyce nodded. "So you might not agree to do the surgery?"

Dr. Reiner sighed. "It's not that I won't do the surgery, but I do encourage my young clients to seriously contemplate why they might want to alter their appearance. They have to know with as much certainty as possible that this is what they want. There are risks involved, as with any kind of surgery. Complications such as infection or a reaction to the anesthesia are possible. Double or blurred vision, asymmetrical healing or scarring are other complicating factors to consider. And the very real possibility that there might not be pixie dust at the end of a hard road to recovery. Not everyone has the same reaction after cosmetic surgery. For some people it's worth it. For others, the results might not be what they expected, or their life doesn't change in the way they want it to. I try and encourage as much thinking and questioning as possible before making the final decision."

"Does it hurt a lot?" Joyce asked in a tiny voice.

Dr. Reiner put his hands up and looked like he was trying to gauge how to catch a football that had just been tossed into the air. "Well, that is a hard question to answer only because people have various levels of tolerance for pain."

"But there is pain."

"Well, yes. Anytime you cut and sew your skin, there will be pain. It's just a matter of how you mentally take on that challenge and also how your body heals. Luckily, the plus side of being a teenager in regard to surgery is the repair rate, which is much faster for young cells like yours."

"Great," Joyce said, without much joy. The part about cutting and sewing was still on her mind. "How much cutting do you have to do?" Joyce could still picture the surgery photos that she had found on the Internet. Her stomach jumped at the image.

"That depends on what procedure you choose to undergo to achieve the crease that you want. Some opt to cut and secure the fold to the tarsal plate, which is the most effective way of making sure the folds do not disappear. Others opt for a laser cut, which has a faster rate of healing. And others, with young skin such as yours, might only need a few stitches to hold the skin back, but there is also a higher possibility that the fold might not stay in place."

Joyce mulled over all the information. "What hurts the least?"

Dr. Reiner smiled. "I take it you have a low level of tolerance for pain."

Joyce grimaced and nodded.

"Well, I would recommend, based on your age and lack of complicating conditions, to try the stitches. Always best to go with the least invasive treatment and see if that works."

"Otherwise, what do you have to do?" Joyce asked.

"We can always go back and operate again."

"Are you going to put me to sleep?"

Dr. Reiner was looking down at his clipboard, filling in some information. "Sleep?"

"Put me under. So I don't feel anything."

"Oh. No. We'll just use local anesthesia."

"You mean I'll be awake for the whole thing?"

"Yes, Joyce. Is that a problem?" Dr. Reiner put down his clipboard and looked very concerned.

"No." Joyce waved her hands. "No. I mean. Can't you just make me go to sleep and then I won't have to worry about anything?"

"There are more risks involved when we fully anesthetize someone. And for a procedure like this, I wouldn't recommend taking any more risks than is necessary."

"Okay," Joyce said weakly.

Dr. Reiner opened up a drawer under the sink counter. He pulled out a hand mirror, which he handed over to Joyce, small tweezers and a bottle filled with some clear liquid. He set all the equipment on the counter and then rolled the small table with the laptop computer over to Joyce.

Dr. Reiner pointed to the sheet with the eyes. "If you'll notice the difference in appearance in each set of eyes. Some choose to have a larger, more defined crease. Where the crease begins and how you want it to taper or not taper off is a very personal decision. I can do any of the creases that you see there on the sheet."

Joyce scanned through all the eyes but didn't really see a difference. Dr. Reiner pointed to one set of eyes.

"This person wanted her crease to be as understated and natural looking as possible. See how narrow the crease is compared to the eyes in this photo. And the ends of this one taper down as opposed to flaring out."

"Oh," Joyce said, finally noticing the difference. "How do you know what looks best on me?"

Dr. Reiner sat up in his chair and reached over for the small table with the laptop. He turned the laptop slightly toward him and punched in a few commands. Magically, Joyce's face appeared on the screen. Dr. Reiner zoomed in on Joyce's eyes. He turned to Joyce.

"It depends on how you want your eyes to look," Dr. Reiner said. He fiddled with the keys and moved the cursor over to Joyce's eyelids. Slowly the image changed so that Joyce could see her eyes opening slightly and a narrow crease appearing where there had been none before. Joyce raised her fingertips to her eyelid as though the same crease was engraving itself into her skin. Dr. Reiner glanced at her and smiled. Joyce pretended she had a bug bite on the side of her face.

"Now, we could make your creases more substantial," he said and manipulated the image some more until Joyce had two very distinguishable lines above her eyes. Joyce gasped. That was really weird looking.

"I would recommend trying for something more subtle, but it depends on your taste."

Joyce stared at the foreign eyes on her face. "Yeah," she said, "I think subtle would be better for me." Joyce thought about the Korean mothers' grapevine going into overdrive when they saw her with huge san-gah-pu-rhees on her face. At least if the line was more natural, people might not notice right away and then they might think the folds had always been there.

Dr. Reiner decreased the size of the crease and let Joyce have a look.

Joyce studied the eyes staring back at her. She stared down at the sheet with all the eyes. The various pairs seemed to be saying pick me, pick me. Moving the sheet of eyes closer then farther then closer to her face, Joyce tried to distinguish the differences between the creases, but ended up feeling overwhelmed. She could feel Dr. Reiner waiting and yet she didn't want to rush and pick just any old pair of eyes. This was worse than trying on clothes at the department store. If only Gina were here.

Dr. Reiner wheeled forward. "Let me suggest trying something for a trial basis. We can glue back part of your eyelids to create the effect of the defined pretarsal crease and then you can see if you would like to go bigger or smaller."

"You can do that?" Joyce said.

Dr. Reiner picked up the small bottle. "Very common in Asian countries for women who do not choose or can't afford the permanent route to glue or tape their eyelids back. It's not unlike women here gluing on fake eyelashes."

"Cool," Joyce said. After a second she added, "There isn't any pain involved?"

Dr. Reiner smiled as he put on his rubber gloves. "No, Joyce."

Dr. Reiner applied a thin layer of glue on one eye and carefully used his tweezers to lift up a portion of the skin on her upper eyelid until Joyce could see a crease forming in the mirror she held up to her face.

"That is so amazing," Joyce said when he was done. She turned from side to side to check out the results. Only one eyelid was up but Joyce could see what a difference it was making. Dr. Reiner held a small ruler to her eye and noted the exact measurement.

"Let's do the other one," Dr. Reiner said and Joyce moved the mirror to one side so that he could do the other eyelid.

Joyce couldn't stop staring at herself in the mirror.

"Wow! This is crazy! I didn't really think a small change would make this big a difference in the way I looked."

Dr. Reiner dropped all his equipment into the sink and threw away his gloves. "The glue should keep your eyelids in place for a day or so. Use warm water and soap if you want to dissolve the glue. And I wouldn't recommend vigorously rubbing your eyes."

"Okay," Joyce said, still reveling in her new appearance. She felt like she was looking at someone she knew but didn't know. Someone familiar and yet different. Who did she look like?

"Joyce," Dr. Reiner said. "Joyce."

Joyce looked up from the mirror.

"So you like what you see?"

Joyce grinned so wide, she worried her creases might pop off. She dialed back the wattage of her smile. "Thank you, Dr. Reiner!"

Dr. Reiner picked up his clipboard. "I'll make a note of the size crease you have and when you come back in for the surgery, we can talk about whether you want to keep it to that size or go bigger or smaller."

"So the next time I see you, I'm going to make this permanent?"

"Only if you decide that is the right decision for you." Dr. Reiner shook Joyce's hand. "It was nice to have met you, Joyce. Why don't you come out after you've had another minute to look at the handout of the different sets of eyes. I'll just check in with your aunt."

He left the handout on the counter before he closed the door. Joyce walked over and picked up the sheet, studying each crease carefully and then comparing it to the crease that she had in her eyelids now. Joyce rejected a few for looking too big and puffy. She noted that the bigger the crease the thicker the skin looked around the eyes. Maybe this is what Sam is doing, Joyce thought. Was he going to put a bunch of shots together of people's faces? Joyce would have to check in with him about what he was going to do with all the photos he was taking of her.

It felt so odd to be looking into a mirror and not feel dissatisfied with her image looking back. Joyce studied her face from all angles and still she couldn't stop grinning. She was stunned by the difference. Stunned at how happy she felt staring at her face. Even her skin looked better with her new eyes. Finally, after she had made as many faces as she could think of—happy, sad, moody, mysterious, alluring—to see how her eyes looked, Joyce set down the mirror and left the examining room. Out in the hallway, she passed the nurse who had checked Joyce in. The nurse gave her a bright smile. Joyce smiled, feeling a zap of confidence pulling back her shoulders, an arrogant swivel swinging her hips as she strolled toward the door. She stepped out into the waiting room.

"Joyce!" Gomo said, standing up. "I knew the procedure would make you look different, but I had no idea it would make you look so much like Helen."

Joyce touched the side of her face. "Helen?"

Gomo walked over to her and stared into Joyce's

eyes. "You look wonderful. Dr. Rie-ne-or said that you were very happy with this preliminary result. How do you like it?"

Joyce stepped away, her hand still touching her temple. So that was why Joyce recognized herself but didn't recognize herself. She whirled around to face Gomo. "Do I really look like Helen now?"

Gomo nodded. "Beautiful."

FOURTEEN

joyce stepped into the apartment and threw open her arms.

"I'm back!" she announced. No one came to greet her. Not even Andy peeked out of his room to make a comment.

Uhmma and Apa had to be at the restaurant, but where were Andy and Helen? Joyce walked to her room. Helen was still in bed, her covers over her head.

Joyce stood at the doorway. "Helen, where's Andy?"

Helen didn't answer.

Joyce walked over to the mirrored closet door and checked her reflection. Her eyes were still amazing. For once, Joyce was excited at the thought of getting ready for the beach. Joyce reached in and pulled out her red tank dress.

"Too bad Dr. Reiner didn't lipo my knees," she said out loud. Well, it didn't matter. She was feeling too good about her face to worry about her knees. Besides, Joyce told herself firmly, she was going to exercise and get rid of the fat pockets.

Helen turned over onto her side. "Are you talking to me?"

"I'm just talking to myself." Joyce stepped away from the closet and waited for Helen to comment on her transformation. Joyce blinked slowly and purposefully.

Helen's mouth twisted to one side. "I see you got your eyes done."

"Actually, these are only temporary, but I have an appointment next month to make them permanent." Joyce stepped toward the mirror to examine the creases. "Do you think I should have the folds be bigger?"

Helen sat up and pushed herself out of bed. "I don't think you should have them done at all."

Joyce frowned. "You know, Helen. You could be just a tad more supportive of me. I mean, ultimately, if it makes me happy, then what's wrong with that?" Joyce said, feeling like she was an echo for a second.

Helen stood up and walked to the door. "There's nothing wrong with being happy, but if it's built on false pretenses, then the only person you're fooling is yourself. I can't believe you would be so superficial in your values."

Joyce whirled around. "Just shut up, Helen. You have no idea what you're talking about. False pretenses. Just because I want to look pretty, I have no values? Why do you always have to be so high and mighty? Who are you to judge me?"

"I'm not judging you. I just think you should give this whole plastic surgery idea some more serious thought. There is no such thing as a miracle cure."

"Oh, so now even a miracle won't save me." Joyce threw up her middle finger. "You know, Helen, I might not be pretty, but I am not the ugliest person out there."

"That's not what I mean. You're in high school. You don't know yourself well enough yet. So many things could change."

"Just because I'm not some goal-oriented dweeb who has wanted to be a doctor all her life doesn't mean I don't know how to make a serious decision."

"Joyce, you're being a drama queen right now. We

can talk about this later. I have to shower or else I'm going to be late for my meeting."

"Well, I need the car, and you said you'd cover for me today," Joyce said firmly.

Helen simply shook her head. "I'll cover for you after my meeting. You have to talk to Uhmma and Apa if you want the car today."

Joyce stared at Helen reflected in the mirror. All the anger she had been harboring was unleashed.

"You know, Helen. You've been a moody, selfish bitch ever since Su Yon left," Joyce shouted. "Maybe she left because she couldn't take being a friend to someone so self-centered. *Maybe* she didn't leave the city at all but left the restaurant so that she could dump you as a friend."

Helen's face froze. She stepped back into the room. "You saw her? But I've searched everywhere. I've driven so many miles."

Joyce pretended she hadn't heard Helen and held up the red dress against her body.

"Please, Joyce. Just tell me where you saw her."

"I need the car."

Helen's eyes narrowed in agitation. "Fine. Take the car. I don't care. Just tell me where you saw her."

"I didn't see her," Joyce said.

Helen crumbled to the ground. "But you just said that you saw her. You just said. You just said you saw her in the city."

Joyce felt guilty for having led Helen on, but still, it served her right. Joyce grabbed the car keys from the top of Helen's dresser and raced into the hallway with her red dress.

"I said *maybe* I saw her," Joyce called out before slamming the bathroom door.

The door to their bedroom was shut when Joyce emerged from the bathroom wearing her red tank dress. She went to call Gina from the kitchen.

"Hey, guess who has the car? I know, I know. I'm going to drive us to that beach volleyball practice. And guess what else? I'm coming over with my new eyes, so get your makeup bag ready." Joyce pulled the phone away from her ear just as Gina shrieked. She hung up the phone and danced her way across the living room and out the door.

Joyce drove down the freeway with the windows open. Her hair whipped up into her face as her spirits soared.

She kept both hands on the steering wheel, two o'clock and ten o'clock, and checked her side view mirrors every few minutes just like she learned in driver's ed. Gina was singing loudly with the radio, one foot sticking out the window. Joyce was grinning so hard she felt her teeth drying out. Gina pointed to Joyce and mimicked taking photos. Joyce tried to pout and preen at Gina, but she didn't want to take her eyes off the road, so it looked more like she was making faces at the car in front of her. But none of that mattered. Joyce was happy to be giggling with her best friend, happy in the knowledge that she looked fabulous. Even her skin was cooperating.

Gina's powder had worked magic to minimize her pores. And her eyes: Joyce had to glance at them in the rearview mirror again. Her eyes were amazing. Gina had lined them with black and spread a little pink shimmering eye shadow around the edges just to draw attention, but didn't go overboard since it was daytime. Gina had also showed Joyce the darker, more dramatic shades for the evening. Some night, like prom, Joyce fantasized that she would wear that makeup. And John would gaze down at her as he held her close in a slow dance, mesmerized by her eyes.

All the stars were in alignment. All the signs pointed

to a perfect day. Joyce checked the rearview mirror to change lanes, and Helen's tropical-colored bags glared out at her for a moment. Joyce refocused her eyes on the road. There was no doubt in Joyce's mind, this summer was going to change her life.

Joyce carefully parked the car. She and Gina stepped out and stood on the boardwalk, ready to find the church group.

"Hey, I see Lisa," Joyce said, pointing to a group at the volleyball net. Gina was adjusting the oversized shades she was wearing to take attention away from her cheeks.

"Can you ask Dr. Reiner next time if they have lipo for people with large cheeks? I mean, you would think the technology was around for something like that," Gina said.

"Yeah, right after he does my fat knees." Joyce stared at her friend, who was suddenly looking anxious. "What are you worried about?"

"Lisa and her friends are all so hot. And you look amazing now. I just don't feel like I'll fit in."

Joyce shook her head. "Don't worry, you look fabulous in that skirt and tank top. Besides, no one accessorizes like you," Joyce said and pointed to the pretty handkerchief knotted casually around Gina's neck.

As they approached the group, Joyce squinted at a figure. "Hey, who is that?"

Gina took off her glasses. "Who?"

The figure turned to the side, and Joyce could see that he was holding a camera in his hands. "I didn't know Sam went to these things," Joyce said.

"Yeah, I called and told him that his model was going to be here," Gina said, walking toward the group.

Joyce ran after her, holding on to the sides of her short dress so that the hem wouldn't ride up. "Gina! I don't want my picture taken. He'll say something about my eyes getting done!"

"I like Sam. He's a good guy. Joyce, stop worrying. Your eyes look great," Gina said. "Be proud!"

Joyce snorted, but she lifted her chin and let go of the sides of her dress. She couldn't wait to show Lisa her new eyes.

Lisa was with a group of her girlfriends standing off to the side of the volleyball court when Gina and Joyce approached. Lisa smiled and waved Joyce over.

"Hi, Joyce," Lisa said. She did a double-take and then gave Joyce a knowing look. Joyce smiled, curling up just one corner of her lips, hoping it looked as mysterious as the smile Lisa had given her on Sunday.

"Hey, Lisa," Joyce said.

"You look fabulous, Joyce," Lisa said, lavishing attention on her. The group also chimed in to say how great Joyce looked.

"That dress looks hot on you," Lisa said.

Joyce looked down at herself. "Thanks! This is my friend Gina," Joyce said and introduced Gina to the others.

Gina stood off to the side, strangely subdued. The more Lisa only talked to Joyce, the more Gina inched away from the group. And though Joyce reached over and tried to pull her closer, Gina resisted.

Lisa continued. "Whenever I wear dresses or shorts that short, I get all hung up on my thighs. You don't seem to have that problem."

At the mention of the word *thigh*, all the other girls began to laugh and shout out their insecurities like a laundry list of chores: freckles, cottage-cheese thighs, flabby arms, double chins, ingrown hairs, zits, small boobs, too large boobs, thin lips.

"I get worried about my knees," Joyce admitted.

Lisa stared down at Joyce's legs. "Huh. Oh, yeah, I see what you mean. Those little fat pockets above the knees. They have this new liposuction technique now where they use a laser."

Joyce felt herself shrinking. She wanted to cross her legs or sit down and cover them with a beach towel. Why had she gone out with this dress on? And red, of all the colors. Could her fat knees be more obvious? Joyce heard the clicking of a camera going off to the side of her.

"Sam, please stop!" Joyce said and tried to block her face with her hand.

"Joyce, Joyce, you're killing me here," Sam said. He stopped taking pictures and came over. "I have to get these shots before the group show. You said you would model."

Joyce stepped away from Lisa and muttered between her clenched teeth, "I said I would help you, but I didn't think that would mean being your model for the rest of my days."

Sam stepped back. "Jeez, Joyce, you don't have to be a jerk about it. If you don't want to pose anymore, just say so. I'll find someone else."

Joyce waved. "Bye, Sam. Find someone else."

Sam held up the camera and fired off one last shot at Joyce's face and then turned and walked away. Joyce held the sides of her dress and scurried back over to Lisa and her group. They were talking and pointing to someone in the water. Gina stood just on the outer edges, listening.

"God, he can be such a stalker," Joyce said to Lisa.

Gina gave Joyce a look, but Joyce pretended she didn't see it.

Lisa was shielding her eyes as she looked out at the ocean. "You have to be careful of who starts crushing on you."

"Oh, no. It's not like that. Sam's just a friend," Joyce said.

Gina coughed. "Yeah, who said Sam has a crush on Joyce?"

Lisa put down her hands and leaned forward to direct her comment at Gina. "It's so obvious that loser is following her around. Last Sunday, I swear, every time I turned around he was taking pictures of her. Does he have to carry his camera around everywhere he goes? Kind of creepy, if you ask me. Who knows what he's posting on the web."

"You have no idea what you're talking about. Sam's an amazing photographer," Gina said, her head snapping to the left. "So step off."

Lisa parted her perfectly lined red lips to return fire at Gina.

"Hey, Lisa," Joyce interrupted her, "you were saying that they have a new laser technique for those hard spots." Joyce pointed to her knees.

Lisa turned away from Gina, who was staring off at the ocean, her arms crossed in front of her chest.

"Yeah," Lisa said, "it's this new technique they've been using in Europe, but it's not approved yet for the United States. Basically, they use a laser to melt the fat smoothly. And they can use it on smaller pockets of fat like above your knees or for people who have a BIG face, suck a little fat from their cheeks."

Gina took off her sunglasses and turned toward Lisa. "Did you just call me fat?"

Lisa snorted. "No. But I see you have some issues, if you thought I was talking about you."

"I heard what you said." Gina's head began to snake around as though about to strike.

Joyce jumped over to Gina. "I don't think Lisa was calling you fat, Gina."

Gina stepped back. "I can't believe you're defending her. She just called Sam a creepy loser, and now you're letting her call me fat."

"She didn't say you were fat, Gina!" Joyce stepped closer to Gina and said in a low voice, "Will you stop with the hysterics? It was just a misunderstanding. She's nice. Just chill out."

Gina threw up her hands and then slipped on her sunglasses. "You know what, Joyce? If getting your eyes done means you're going to hang out with someone like her, I'm finished here." Gina walked away.

Joyce started to go after her, but she heard Lisa gasp. Joyce turned around. Lisa was shielding her eyes again and looking out at the ocean.

"He is SO gorgeous," Lisa said, pointing to a figure in the distance.

Joyce followed Lisa's finger. All thoughts of finding Gina vanished. There was only room for three words in Joyce's mind. John Ford Kang.

john Ford Kang emerged from the waves like a surfing god. He flipped his head back, and his wet hair flew off his forehead. He carried his surfboard under one arm as he ran onto the beach and then set it down next to his towel. Bits of seaweed clung to his muscular chest.

Joyce could feel her mouth hanging open. She turned to Lisa, who was staring as openly as Joyce was.

"You know him?" Joyce asked, forcing her eyes to peel off of his smooth, tanned skin.

"Yeah. His father works with my uncle over at a software firm." Lisa's eyes openly devoured him. "Too bad his mom and dad are in the middle of splitting up."

"Really?" Joyce said.

Lisa lowered her voice and spoke out of the corner of her lips. "She was caught cheating with this English guy at work. It's kind of sad, actually. John and his father really embraced his mother's side of the family and traveled to Germany every vacation to be with them. They seem kind of lost now without her, but my uncle has been trying to get them to try more Korean things. You know, go to church and see more of the Korean side of the family. Be a part of the Korean fold."

A faint ringing could be heard. Lisa took her cell phone out of her pocket and checked the screen.

"I have to take this call. You should go up and introduce yourself to him as my friend." Lisa held the phone to her ear and stepped away from Joyce.

Joyce continued standing there, wondering what to do. In the distance, she could see Sam and Gina walking away from the volleyball area. A few of the guys who were practicing their volleyball serves were calling out to John. Joyce couldn't take her eyes off him. John glanced up.

Joyce froze.

John waved.

Joyce turned around to see if he was waving at someone else standing behind her. She turned back around, and John was still waving. Joyce tentatively held up her hand and waved her fingers a bit. John smiled. Joyce wiggled her fingers more forcefully. She wiggled her fingers better than any cheerleader doing spirit fingers. What was she supposed to do next? What would Lisa do?

"Go talk to him," Joyce muttered to herself. But her feet wouldn't move, and her fingers just kept on writhing like busy little worms. I have to stop, she thought as her hand began to cramp up, but her fingers had become disconnected from her mind and kept on wagging.

John started walking toward her. Joyce immediately dropped her eyes only to realize that her chubby knees were showing. Joyce grabbed her skirt and tried forcing down the hem.

"Hi," John said.

Joyce froze, her hands still clutching her skirt. "Hi," she croaked, looking up at him.

"I didn't know you went to these church events."

Joyce forced her hands off her skirt. "I don't normally. I mean, not that I don't like to, or anything." Joyce remembered what Lisa had said about John and his father trying to get back in touch with their culture. "It's a great way to meet up with Korean friends."

"Right," John said, looking around at the group

gathering to play volleyball. "I don't know many people here."

"Oh," Joyce said, pretending to be surprised.

John turned back to her. "It was great seeing you the other night at your restaurant."

"What?" Joyce said. "At the restaurant?" Had he seen her hanging out of the kitchen doorway looking like the fool?

John gazed down at her, puzzled.

"You met my dad and my uncles and aunts. Come on, Helen, your memory was never this bad in council meetings."

Joyce recalled how he and Helen had hugged. "Oh, wow, okay." Joyce started to laugh. "You thought I was Helen!"

John flicked his hair back again.

"I'm Joyce." She pointed her thumb at herself.

"Who?"

"Helen's sister. Joyce."

John studied her face closely. He stepped back and studied her entire body. Closely. Joyce glanced away for a second when she felt her face burning. He had thought she was Helen. Maybe she shouldn't have corrected him.

"Joyce?" John said.

Joyce straightened her shoulders and reminded herself that she looked just as good as Helen. Even Gomo had said so. Joyce tilted her head slightly and turned to John with her eyes wide and open. "We had AP Chem together."

John stepped forward. "You were in my chem class?"

"Yeah, you even signed my yearbook."

John gazed down at her, a small flirt of a smile brushing up the corners of his lips. He stepped closer. "Wait, did I run into you on the last day?"

Joyce stepped closer. "You knocked me over!" She raised her finger and poked his smooth, sharply defined shoulder. Joyce felt faint, but she remained standing. She wanted to pinch herself. No, she wanted to pinch him. Or at least poke his shoulder again. Joyce couldn't believe she was actually flirting with John Ford Kang.

"That was you!" John said, throwing back his head in laughter. "Damn."

"What do you mean?" Joyce said, pretending to be hurt.

"You just look so different."

Joyce jutted out her hip and placed her hand there for emphasis. She watched John's eyes move from her hip to her chest, which made Joyce inhale and exhale quickly to get that nice upward heave, and then his eyes moved to meet her eyes. Joyce blinked slowly, letting the full effect of her shimmering eye shadow do its job. Cool as any blonde at Orangedale, except for her armpits, where Joyce could feel the nervous sweat pooling like a hot springs. Joyce clamped her upper arms to her sides and leaned back to gaze up at his face.

"I think you need glasses or something." Joyce pouted. "You signed my yearbook for Lynn Song."

John's eyes scrunched together. "Lynn? Is she the one who always has her hair hanging in her face?"

Joyce thought about the last day of school and the huge zit that she had been trying to cover with her hair. And the way Lynn's hair kept falling forward as they washed the beakers. So it wasn't really Joyce that he saw that day. He didn't think, technically, that she was ugly, but had mistaken her for Lynn because of the hair in her face.

Joyce gazed up at John Ford Kang, meeting his large brown-green eyes with her own perfectly folded eyes. He was everything she had dreamed. Imagined. Wished for all year long. It was finally happening. To Joyce! She could feel the energy surging from his powerfully built body, felt the pull of his laughter as he joked about Mr. Blevins and leaned in so close that Joyce could smell the sea on his skin! They were talking like they really knew each other. Magic. Lisa Yim had been right. The fold was not about how you looked so much as how it made you feel and act. Was this really the same Joyce, laughing like she had wind chimes for vocal cords? Joyce didn't even know she could make that noise. Joyce's spirits lifted high and fast as the volleyball that sailed over the net.

"Hey, John," the guy who had just served called out. "You going to play or just flirt with all the pretty ladies?"

"I'll be right there," John called back.

The guy sounded a wolf whistle loud enough to make Joyce blush.

"I love you too, Eddie," Lisa Yim called out, walking up to Joyce. "Hey, I'm glad you two met."

Lisa slid right up to John and leaned against his chest.

"Did you know that Helen, I mean, Joyce and I were in the same chemistry class?" John said, stepping back.

"Really?" Lisa said, stepping even closer and staring up into his face. "And you two never met?"

Joyce studied how Lisa curved her body toward John.

Lisa cooed, "I can't believe you two were in the same class without realizing it."

"Well, you and I have known each other for over a year, and we didn't really become friends until two weeks ago," John said.

Lisa laughed and lightly traced the muscles on John's chest. "Yeah, that's true."

A spike of pain shot through Joyce's shoulders, making them slump forward. Her jutted hip collapsed into a slouch. Joyce could feel the tears welling in the corners of her eyes. As quickly as her heart had soared, she could feel the crush of humiliation descending on her. It had to be a mistake. Lisa was just being affectionate. Joyce pretended some sand had blown into her face.

"Man, the wind is really kicking today," Joyce said and turned away to rub the tears from her eyes. John wouldn't have been so flirtatious with her if he were going out with someone else. Especially when that someone had been standing just a few steps away. But, then again, Helen did say he was a player.

Joyce stood there rubbing her eye while her mind whirled and attached to John's last words. Friends. He didn't say girlfriend. He said friends. That was it. Lisa and John were family friends. Of course, his father

and her uncle worked together and probably socialized together. Why wouldn't old friends be affectionate
with each other? Joyce had just been imagining things.
Like always. Joyce shook herself from her reverie. Lisa
and John were just friends, she convinced herself.

"Come on, playboy," Eddie called from the net.

John waved at Eddie and untangled himself from
Lisa's tentacles.

"See you later, ladies," John said. "I have to go kick
some kimchi fool loving ass."

Joyce smiled brightly. "Kick some butt, John!"

John gazed intently at Joyce. "Are your eyes
okay?"

"What?" Joyce nervously raised her fingertips to
the outer edges of her eyes. "Yeah, I just got some sand
in them."

"Go help Eddie before he has a heart attack," Lisa
said and gave him a push.

John ran over to the volleyball game.

Lisa turned to Joyce and whispered urgently, "Your
right eyelid fell!"

"Damn!" Joyce quickly covered that eye.

"I thought you had the procedure done for real. I
was wondering how you had healed so quickly."

Joyce uncovered her eye but kept her head down.

"Dr. Reiner just glued them back so we could see what size crease I wanted."

"Well, do you have more of the glue? I could help you put it back."

"No," Joyce said. "I should get home anyway."

"Too bad you can't stay for the barbecue," Lisa said, watching the game. "Oh, God, even though he's still in high school, he's so gorgeous, it doesn't even matter."

"What doesn't matter?" Joyce asked, glumly staring at the sand.

"That he likes me," Lisa stated.

Joyce rubbed her eyes and then yanked down her skirt some more.

SIXTEEN

joyce trudged back through the sand, holding her skirt in place. Gina and Sam were nowhere to be seen. They probably left, Joyce thought miserably and unlocked the car door. She stepped inside, indifferent to the sand she was tracking in. What had started out as an amazing adventure was beginning to feel like a bad burn day at the beach. A cranky tiredness overwhelmed her body. Joyce checked her eyes in the rearview mirror. Her face looked lopsided with her one eyelid undone. Lopsided and tired and ugly. She tried pulling the other eyelid down, but it held fast.

"Ow, ow, oww!" Joyce stopped pulling, worried she might rip her skin. This was so typical. Everything always backfired. Joyce started up the car. Maybe this was a bad sign. Joyce couldn't even get her eyes done without it failing miserably. And yet, Joyce thought, if it was permanent, her eyelid wouldn't have fallen. She could have stayed for the barbecue and talked to John some more. What made Lisa so sure that he liked her? Joyce started to get fired up. She, not Lisa, would be the one who got to see John every day of the week when school started. Joyce frantically counted the weeks before school started. Her plan could still work. Now, if she could only get the surgery scheduled sooner rather than later. Lisa didn't have a patent out on John. He had been stalking Helen, and now he could come after Joyce. He had flirted with her, right? Joyce rubbed her eye. What if she had been imagining things? If only she could talk to Gina.

As Joyce was inching out of her parking spot, she saw Gina and Sam approaching the lot. Joyce stopped the car and waved frantically at them. Gina abruptly turned around. Sam gazed at Joyce for a second and then did the same. Joyce's hand fell. She couldn't believe Gina and Sam were going to make such a big deal out of nothing. How was she supposed to change if her friends couldn't be supportive? Gina had been the one pushing her to get the surgery in the first place, and now Gina was making her choose between their friendship or her new self? Joyce carefully finished backing up and headed out of the parking lot. The empty car echoed with the sound of Joyce's sniffling. Maybe having a car was overrated.

Joyce walked into the apartment complex just as the sun was beginning to descend. The tall palm trees waved in the pink-orange skies. Joyce walked through the courtyard, her mind still on Gina and Sam, the image of their backs to Joyce lingering in her thoughts. As she approached the stairs leading up to the apartment, she spotted Helen sitting halfway up, wearing her work clothes, staring off into the sky. The sight of her older sister sitting all alone echoed the deep sense of isolation that Joyce felt. How many times this summer had she seen Helen sitting alone like that? Joyce had written it off as Helen being moody, but now she had some idea of how Helen might be feeling. All the ugliness Joyce had shown earlier in the day flooded back to her.

"Hi," Joyce said tentatively, wondering if Helen was still angry.

Helen's eyes lifted up, but her chin remained cradled in the palm of her hand. "Hi."

Joyce started up the stairs. Helen scooted over to make room for Joyce to pass, but instead of heading up to the apartment, Joyce sat down next to her.

"You're not going in to work?" Joyce asked.

"I was just about to go, but then Uhmma called and said there was someone who had answered the ad in the paper. She's training with Apa right now and so I don't have to be there until a little later." Helen smiled faintly, glancing down at the sand on Joyce's flip-flops. "How was the beach?"

Joyce shrugged. "Lame."

Helen remained silent.

"Sorry about taking off with the car earlier," Joyce whispered. "Did you miss your meeting?"

"Yeah," Helen said. "But it was okay."

"Are you sure?" Joyce asked. "You're not going to get kicked off the research group?"

"I wish," Helen said, smiling.

"What?" Joyce was alarmed. This didn't sound like Joyce's high-achieving sister.

"I don't know if I'm cut out for all this doctor stuff."

"Oh, come on, Helen, you have the best psychobabble of anyone I know."

"Thanks, but it doesn't matter how I say things, it's about whether I have the passion to really dedicate myself to the profession, and I don't know if my heart is in it anymore. I'm realizing more and more that being a doctor might not be for me."

"Have you told Uhmma and Apa?" Joyce worried. Her parents had been talking about Helen being the doctor in the family for as long as Joyce could remember.

Helen shook her head.

Joyce wondered how her parents were going to react to Helen's news. They would probably be disappointed, but they would get over it. Joyce hoped they wouldn't start looking at her to take over the doctor role. Joyce had gotten an A in AP Chemistry. Darn, why had she felt the need to compete with Helen and show her parents that she was just as good in the sciences?

"What does any of that matter when I don't even know who I am anymore?" Helen whispered so softly that Joyce barely heard her.

Joyce turned to Helen. "And I'm sorry about lying and saying that I might have seen Su Yon."

At the sound of Su Yon's name, Helen closed her eyes and her lower lip began to tremble. It was so physical, the pain pooling in Helen's face, Joyce could hardly stand to watch. How long had Helen been suffering like this? Joyce put her arm around Helen's shoulders.

"It hurts so much," Helen sobbed.

"It's okay, Helen. Shhh," Joyce said. "It'll be okay."

"I don't know what to do."

"Uhmma and Apa won't care," Joyce said. "Hell, I could be the next doctor. Don't worry, Helen."

Helen hid her face in her hands. "Oh, Joyce, you are so clueless sometimes."

"What?" Joyce pulled back. "I was just trying to help. You don't think I could be a doctor? Well, guess what grade I got in AP Chem."

Helen lowered her hands. "Joyce, it's not about being a doctor."

Joyce frowned. "Well, what is it, then? Are you missing Su Yon?"

Helen stared at the pool for a minute and then glanced at Joyce. "Su Yon and I were really close, Joyce."

"I know," Joyce said.

"I was in love with her."

Joyce stood up quickly. "What do you mean in love?"

Helen craned her head back to see Joyce's face. "I loved her."

Joyce ran down to the bottom of the stairs. She looked back at Helen, who had tears streaming down her cheeks. Joyce ran up the stairs. "You're saying love. Love. Not love like friend love, but love, love."

Helen nodded.

Joyce took a few steps down the stairs. "This is huge. This is so deep." Joyce turned around. "Do Uhmma and Apa know?"

Helen nodded.

"Uhmma and Apa knew all this time, and no one told me? What is going on? Why didn't you tell me?"

Helen shook her head. "I tried to tell you a few times, but you were always angry at me or preoccupied with your own problems. I didn't get a chance to really sit down with you."

Joyce paced at the bottom of the stairs. She looked up at Helen. Her sister was gay? This was crazy. Gay? Joyce didn't know one single gay person. Well, that wasn't true. Their old youth pastor, Paul, had come out about two years ago, but everyone had known he was gay even before he had told them. And they all admired how hard he worked to help his friends who were dying of AIDS. In fact, the entire youth group had held a fund-raiser to help Paul in his efforts. But this was Helen. Helen was gay. How did Joyce miss this? What had she been doing all this time? Mooning over John. Running around with Gina. Ignoring Helen, Joyce thought with guilt.

"Joyce," Helen said, waving her over.

Joyce walked back up the stairs and sat at Helen's feet.

"Joyce, nothing about me is different."

"I know," Joyce said, looking down at the courtyard.

"Joyce, look at me," Helen said.

Joyce glanced up at Helen.

"Hey, it's still me." Helen's long black hair was pulled back in her usual work ponytail, the white shirtsleeves rolled up to her elbows. Her face was clean and pale, without a trace of makeup. Joyce knew this face. Knew she loved Helen even through all the complaining and fighting. Helen would always be her uhn-nee.

"I know it's still you, Helen," Joyce said. She stood up and moved over to sit on the same step as Helen.

"Joyce, when Su Yon left, I finally had to face what I had been feeling for so long. I think I buried myself in my studies so that I could cut that whole romantic side of me off."

"Did Uhmma and Apa make Su Yon leave?" Joyce asked, remembering how sad Su Yon had been that day, saying good-bye at the restaurant.

"No," Helen said. "Su Yon didn't want to deal with me anymore. She was confused, and being around me wasn't helping. And I think her mother started to wonder what was going on between us."

"How did Uhmma and Apa find out?"

"I told them," Helen said.

"Damn, Helen, no taking the easy road for you," Joyce said. She had to admire Helen for her guts. Joyce would have just lied and snuck around rather than face telling her parents something so difficult.

"I couldn't lie anymore," Helen said. "It was killing me."

"How are they handling it?"

Helen smiled. "Uhmma didn't even blink. She said she had already sensed it."

Joyce laughed. "Uhmma and her psychic powers."

"And Apa doesn't know what to say to me anymore. He starts coughing and getting all red every time any of it vaguely comes up. He's trying to read about having gay children like he'll figure out how to fix the car or something."

"No way! So that's the mystery book Apa has been toting around with him all this time."

Helen nodded.

"He is such a dork," Joyce said. Apa had been the first one to learn English by studying on his own late at night. Even as kids, before they could even read, Apa had amassed books by buying them cheap at garage sales. He believed books had all the answers.

"But I don't want anyone to know yet," Helen whispered. "Especially Gomo."

Joyce groaned. "Well, that dating service she gave you says a lot."

"You think she already suspects?" Helen wondered.

"Well, every special gift that Gomo gave us was about improving ourselves, whether we thought we needed improvement or not."

"I know," Helen said. "She thinks dating will help me grow up and stop being so tied to my friends. Maybe I should go out with Mr. Moon again. Maybe it'll change me. Plastic surgery for the heart."

"No," Joyce said, horrified. "Why would you want to do that to yourself?"

A passing cloud shadowed Helen's face. "Wouldn't it just be easier to fake it? Then everyone would be happy. Uhmma and Apa wouldn't have to worry about how all the talk would affect the family. Gomo could keep holding me up as the Korean poster girl."

"And you would be miserable," Joyce said.

Helen shrugged. "It's all about appearances, Joyce. You know that."

Joyce touched her right fallen eyelid fold. Helen frowned.

"Look at how Gomo treats you," Helen said. "I

mean, honestly, giving a teenager plastic surgery is demented. It's not enough that we're bombarded with images of beauty every day through the media, but our own family member says that we can only look pretty if we alter our face in a certain way. It's so ridiculous!"

"Helen, stop." Joyce touched her sister's arm, but Helen was just getting started.

"You know, I should just move away. Why do I live at home? I'll transfer up to Berkeley or something. Screw the Korean grapevine. Screw Gomo! I'm done being the good girl. I am so tired of always being the responsible one. The nice Korean girl who takes care of her family first. I should have just gone to that East Coast women's school, even if it had meant taking money from Gomo. That would have been priceless. Gomo paying for me to hang out with other girls!"

Joyce focused on the cement steps. So that was why Helen had chosen to stay home. She had sacrificed to help her family instead of doing what she wanted.

"Sorry," Helen said, finally cooling down. "Sometimes I feel like nothing is really mine. Like I've been living my whole life trying to please others."

"Yeah," Joyce said softly.

Helen turned to Joyce and touched her fallen eyelid. "Don't alter yourself so that you can fit in, Joyce. You are beautiful on your own."

"How come it doesn't feel that way?" Joyce wondered, staring up at the darkening sky.

"It's hard to feel all right about yourself when everything around you is saying that you have to look a certain way, act and love a certain way. Or buy this product or take this pill and it will make you better. Make you happy. It's all bull. The amazing and hard fact is that there is no magic pill or procedure or anything. What might make you happy one minute might not make you happy the next. What is beautiful now won't be later. Everything is always changing. You have to know what is true to you. Know who you are and what matters the most to you in here," Helen said and pointed to her heart.

"But what if you don't know?" Joyce wondered.

"You're asking me?" Helen laughed.

Joyce laughed as well. "I always thought you had it easy because you knew exactly what you wanted to be, and you were always good at everything you did."

"Oh, Joyce, I knew how to make other people happy. I didn't know how to make myself happy until I fell in love with Su Yon. And then she left me," Helen said. "And here I am back to square one. Still trying to find out what's true to me."

"But you always seemed so confident about everything," Joyce said.

"Just because I was cocky didn't mean I knew what would make me happy. I just did a really good job of covering up,"

"Speaking of covering up, does Andy know?" Joyce asked.

"Andy, the spy? Are you kidding me? Andy was the first to find out. He used to sneak up on me and Su Yon all the time. He said he would stay quiet if I drove him and his buddies to the basketball courts this summer."

"That little blackmailer."

Helen laughed. "It was kind of nice to see Andy so unfazed by it all. Inside information is still inside information to Andy, no matter what the subject."

"So are you really going to keep it all quiet? Are you going to move? What are you going to do?"

Helen went back to cradling her chin in her hand. "I don't know, Joyce. Honestly, I need this summer to think and figure out my next step. I don't want to rush into a decision because I'm feeling pressure. I need to do some soul-searching and know myself a little more. Know what I need. But the last thing I need from anyone right now is drama. So, yes, I want to keep it quiet until I'm ready to make my next move. And by then,

I'll have a better idea of what I want to do. And it won't be based on what other people want for me, that's for sure."

Joyce nodded.

Helen stood up. "I should get to the restaurant."

"What about Gina?" Joyce asked.

Helen took a step down and turned around. "Gina has a big mouth, Joyce."

"I know, I know," Joyce said. "But she's my best friend."

"I don't know that I can trust her, Joyce," Helen said.

"She means well," Joyce said.

Helen tapped the metal banister with her nails. "If you say so."

"I've always told her everything."

"But she's not family, Joyce. She doesn't understand or even have the same concerns or issues as we do. That was one thing that I learned from this whole mess with Su Yon. Before she left, I trusted her completely." Helen winced. "But Su Yon wouldn't even stay long enough to give me an explanation. She was just gone. And you know who tried to cheer me up? Gomo. She bought me those awful tropical book bags. As bad as Gomo can be sometimes, in her own crazy, demented way, she tries to

look after us. And someday we'll be there for her w
she needs us. That is what a family does. We watch ᴏᴜₜ
for each other. We take care of each other. Are you sure
Gina would do that for you?"

Joyce couldn't answer Helen. She thought about
Gina turning her back to Joyce.

"Will it kill you not to say something about me?"
Helen asked.

"I guess not."

"It's really important to me, Joyce. When I'm ready,
you can be the first one to tell her, okay?"

"Okay," Joyce said and stood up.

Helen ran back up the stairs and embraced her sister. "Thanks, Joyce, for understanding."

SEVENTEEN

joyce found it easier not to call Gina rather than be tempted to tell her such a big secret. She had given Helen her word, and for once, Joyce wanted to make sure that she was doing the right thing by Helen. So Joyce didn't call, and Gina didn't call her either. Joyce was mostly at the restaurant on busy weekend nights and occasionally at lunchtime since they hired the new waitress, but the rest of the days were meant for SAT studying, summer reading and making sure Andy stayed out of trouble.

Gina and Joyce hadn't had a fight this bad since fifth grade, when Joyce hit Gina in the eye with a pillow and said that it was Gina's fault for starting the pillow fight. Joyce wondered if Mrs. Lee knew everything. She was always around the kitchen, and she and Uhmma were as close as any two sisters.

Joyce moped around the apartment all week, checking email and the phone messages, hoping Gina would break the ice. Sometimes, when the apartment was completely empty, Joyce would go to the back of her closet and drag out the yearbook John signed. She felt instantly pathetic, but she couldn't help it sometimes, she just needed to look. Joyce had crossed out Lynn's name and written her own name above it. She stared at his handwriting, studied his sentences as though they might magically decode themselves into a secret message for her. Most times, reading his note made her feel worse, but every once in a while, if she scanned the entry quickly with her eyes squinted, she could almost convince herself that he had written it all for her.

Uhmma and Apa both acknowledged in their own way that Helen had spoken to Joyce.

Apa showed Joyce his book. "I am almost at the end. I still do not understand everything, but I will try and answer your questions," he said like some professor.

Joyce smiled awkwardly and backed away. The last people she wanted to talk to about sexuality were her parents. "That's okay, Apa. Maybe you could find me a book."

Apa's eyes lit on fire at the thought. "Good idea!"

Uhmma spoke in dream references, trying to convince herself and Joyce that she had known all along this was in the future for Helen. "Your sister is the same sister you have always had."

"I know, Uhmma," Joyce said, trying to walk away.

Uhmma followed after her and continued her story. "When Helen was just a baby in my womb, I had a dream about her. I was in a field of flowers, and I reached down to pick one to put in my hair and noticed one flower that was colored very brilliantly but was so unusual and turned almost inside out. I still chose the flower for its great beauty, but I knew this flower would face a different road from all the others."

"Okay, Uhmma," Joyce said and raced to the bathroom. "I have to wash my face."

Andy had digested the news long ago and was on to more pressing problems. Shark liver extract problems. The side effect was not disappearing, and it kept Andy close to home. Not even playing his video games helped his mood.

Andy kicked one of Joyce's beauty magazines that was lying on the floor.

"You are such a crab," Joyce muttered, picking up the magazine. "Would you just stop taking the pills?"

Andy turned away, but Joyce could tell by his tight-fitting jeans that he was wearing more than just his normal tighty whities.

"It's none of your business, so you can go back to moping around the house waiting for Gina to call," Andy said.

Joyce scowled and plopped down on the couch with her magazine. "For your information, I was not waiting for Gina to call," she reported.

"Whatever you say, Joyce." Andy got himself a soda from the refrigerator. Joyce watched him pull out a small yellow capsule from his pocket and swig it down with his drink.

Joyce pretended that she was reading her magazine and asked casually, "Andy, did you ever think that maybe the pills weren't what made Tom Koh grow last summer?"

Andy walked over to the living room window and stared out, sipping his drink. After a moment, he argued, "But we were exactly the same height last summer. And then he took those pills and grew five inches. Now he always gets past me on the courts."

Joyce sighed. She hated to do this to him, but he had to get a clue sometime. "Did you ever think that maybe Tom just went through puberty?"

Andy shrieked and turned around, a look of horror distorting his features. He shrank back from Joyce as though she was holding a crucifix and a wreath of garlic.

"No," he spat, his eyes bulging, his lips curled back in pain.

Joyce nodded. "Yes, Andy."

Andy grabbed one side of his head as though the information Joyce had just presented was about to make his mind explode. "That doesn't make any sense."

"Didn't Tom's voice get deep?" Joyce pointed out.

"But he had a summer cold."

"That lasted all year long?"

Andy turned away.

"And isn't Tom getting a dark shadow on his upper lip?"

"He's just extra tan from being on the courts all day. Now that he can do layups, he thinks he's the next Kobe or something."

Joyce pounded in the last nail. "And he's been hanging out with Suzi Kim a lot at church."

Andy covered his ears and began yelling, "Shut up, shut up, shut up."

Joyce went back to her magazine. "I'm just saying, you have to look at all the evidence."

"I don't want to talk about it anymore."

"Maybe you should lay off the pills for a while."

"I don't want to talk about it."

"And then you won't have to wear five layers of underwear."

Andy scowled. "Joyce, I'm gonna get you back. You won't know how or when. But I'm going to get you." Andy wrinkled his nose and made his fingers into a gun, pulling the trigger. He slowly turned back to the window and continued to drink his soda. After a moment, he reached down and adjusted the seat of his jeans. "I'm gonna go help Sam fill up the pool," Andy said.

"Sam is filling up the pool?" Joyce sat up. "But it's filled with cement."

Andy let out an exasperated grunt. "It's a kiddie pool, Joyce."

The two of them went down to investigate. Sam was standing over the inflatable pool with a garden hose and watching the water slowly inch up the sides.

"Hey," Joyce said softly, hoping Sam wasn't still mad at her.

"Hey," Sam said and glanced at her quickly with a smile.

"Can I fill up my water gun?" Andy asked, still sipping his soda.

"Sure," Sam said.

Andy ran back upstairs and then quickly emerged with two water guns. He ran across the upper hallway and banged on a neighbor's door. The Changs' oldest boy, Jason, who was two years younger than Andy, answered and immediately came outside to play.

Sam filled the pool to the very top. While the boys filled their guns, Sam went back into his apartment and emerged holding two folding beach chairs. He set them up next to the pool and gestured for Joyce to take a seat.

"Thanks," Joyce said and sat down. She carefully rolled up the cuffs of her jeans.

Andy and Jason raced over to the planters that covered the area where the old pool used to be and began to squirt water at each other as they used the plants for camouflage.

Sam sat down in the other chair and flicked off his flip-flops before planting his feet in the water. "Now, that is what a pool is for," he said and leaned back in his chair.

"Tough day?" Joyce asked and gingerly placed her feet into the cold water.

"Just a lot of running around for no pay," Sam said.

Joyce kicked her feet around, making small waves that breached the walls of the small pool and darkened the cement.

"Are you still working on your group show?"

"Yeah." Sam nodded. "It's next week."

Joyce stared at her feet. "Sorry about the other day, at the beach. I was terrible." Joyce turned to Sam. "I'll let you take those photos of my face if you still need them."

Sam clasped his hands together behind his head as though considering her offer. Finally he said, "Nah. It's okay." He gazed down at the pool and wiggled his toes in the water. "It took me a while to stop being mad at you," he said quietly.

Joyce watched Andy nail Jason in the face with some water. "I wasn't myself that day," Joyce said lamely. "I had some issues going on."

Sam nodded. "Gina told me."

Joyce frowned and sat up in her seat, turning to Sam.

"What did Gina say, exactly?" Joyce felt her suspicion growing. Maybe Helen was right. There was no way to trust Gina.

Sam scrunched up his face for a moment and then said, "She told me everything."

"Everything? Everything?" Joyce asked. "Like eyes everything?"

Sam nodded.

Joyce slouched back. "Gina has a big mouth. I swear. Nothing is a secret with her. She just shares everyone's business."

Sam unclasped his hands. "Wait, Joyce," Sam said, leaning over to her. "Don't be mad at Gina."

"Why not?" Joyce asked, kicking the water. "I don't care how mad she was at me. She shouldn't have said anything."

"She wasn't mad," Sam explained. "She was hurt. She was sad and needed someone to talk to. I don't even think she meant to say anything, but I had already kind of figured it out."

Joyce sighed. "You could tell?"

Sam gave her a gentle smile. "Joyce, I'm a photographer. Don't you think I would notice something that different about your face?" Sam turned away from Joyce and stared intently at his naked feet in the water. "Especially your face."

Joyce felt herself blushing. "So what did Gina say about me?" Joyce asked, keeping her eyes on her feet.

"Mostly we trashed you," Sam said.

Joyce jerked her head up in alarm.

Sam grinned. "Just kidding. Honestly, I spent most of the time listening to Gina be worried that she might lose you as a friend."

"What?" Joyce said. "How could she think that? I mean, we've been best friends for years. I would never abandon Gina."

"I think Gina was more concerned that you might outgrow her. The way you acted at the beach really freaked her out. What if you decided to trade up in the friendship category, too?"

"Oh." It was so odd getting secondhand information about her best friend. She was used to sharing her problems with Gina, not hearing about how Gina was having a problem with her. Joyce leaned forward and let her hands drag through the water, watching the circles of swells radiate out. All those hoops that Gina had set up, and she had jumped through them like an obedient pet.

Joyce sat up and muttered angrily, "Gina was the one who wanted me to get my eyes done. I don't understand how she could be threatened by something she wants for me. So which version of Gina's story am I supposed to believe? This is just like her."

"I think she's scared of losing you," Sam said. "It's not that she doesn't want the best for you, because she does, Joyce."

"Really?" Joyce asked, sitting back.

Sam nodded. "She thinks you look great with those things." Sam pointed to his eyes. "But she doesn't want you to change because of them."

Joyce let the information sink in, taking her back to the day at the beach when everything seemed to be going perfectly. Except it wasn't perfect with Gina or Helen or even John, for that matter. Joyce thought about how loud the sound of her sniffling had been in the empty car as she drove home from the beach. So different from the ride over with Gina.

"I guess I was getting pretty obsessed with the way I looked."

Sam shrugged. "We all care about how we look. But when it takes over your life and you start acting weird, I don't know. Is it worth it?"

Joyce grabbed her long hair and pulled it back off her face. Was it worth it? All that attention from John, the confidence she felt talking to him. Two little folds on her eyelids had changed Joyce's world. Was it worth it? And what if Helen was right? Everything is always changing. What if the folds stopped working their magic? Would she want to change her knees or her skin next? Was getting her eyes done really that important? Was that really true to who she was?

"I'm so confused. I don't know what to do. Do I get my eyes done? Do I talk to Gina? What should I do, Sam?"

"I should tell you"—Sam took a deep breath and forced his eyes from the water to meet Joyce's eyes—"I don't know if I'm best person to ask about that."

"Why?" Joyce asked and then regretted asking. What if Lisa Yim was right? What if Sam did have a crush on her? Joyce wanted to jump out of her chair and flee upstairs just to avoid the confrontation. Where was Andy when she needed a little distraction? He and Jason had disappeared.

Sam fiddled with the arms of his chair and finally admitted, "'Cause I'm on these serious meds for my acne."

"Ohhhh," Joyce said, relieved.

"I'm a little embarrassed by it all, but Gina said I shouldn't be. It took me a long time to decide to do it, but I was so tired of always feeling self-conscious. I definitely chose to do something about the way I looked, so I can't really say whether you should do something to improve your looks or not. I think you look fine, great, without the folds, but then I don't have a problem with your eyes. And you might. And if they bug you that much, then maybe you should do something about them."

Joyce appreciated Sam's honesty. "You know, the whole fold thing didn't even cross my mind until my Gomo offered the surgery." Joyce grinned. "And then I couldn't get it off my mind. Everyone's eyes just jumped out at me. Did she have the fold? Did she get the surgery? Know what I mean?"

Sam smiled. "Yeah, it's like me and skin. I notice everyone's complexion even before their eyes."

"Yeah!" Joyce said, relieved someone understood.

Sam grinned widely and pulled some lip balm from his hip pocket. He held it up before uncapping it and applied some to his lips. "One of the side effects of my meds is that I get really dry skin and chapped lips. Gina took me to that department store she works at and bought me this lip stuff."

Joyce clapped. "She made you walk around the makeup counters with her!"

"She knows where everything is," Sam said, shaking his head and recapping the lip balm.

"I know." Joyce laughed.

"She could be dangerous," Sam said.

"Yeah."

"We'll have to keep her away from the dark side." Sam slid the lip balm back in his pocket. "This stuff really works. My lips feel better already."

Joyce snuck a peek at Sam leaning back in his striped beach chair, his hands comfortably clasped on top of his stomach, his lips slick with moisturizer. He had said "we" as though they were Gina's closest friends. As though he was already in her life.

Joyce's sixth sense went into overdrive.

"Have you and Gina been talking a lot lately?" Joyce asked as casually as possible.

"Yeah," Sam said, not catching her eyes. He couldn't help himself. A second later, a small smile opened his face. "When she does that Godzilla thing"—Sam chuckled at the memory—"man, I almost peed my pants laughing the first time she did that imitation. I was the biggest Godzilla fan when I was, like, eight or nine."

Joyce broke out into laughter. "She is SO cute when she does that!"

"Yeah," Sam said, still smiling to himself. "I make her say that line every time we see each other."

"I see," she said and leaned back into her beach chair. Joyce smiled to herself as she felt the sun sinking into her body. She couldn't wait to pry all the details from Gina. Joyce noticed a light sprinkling of drops hit the cement. She glanced up at the sky, wondering if it was starting to rain.

Andy and Jason stood on the second-floor landing, shooting their water guns and trying not to laugh hysterically.

"Nice try, Andy," Joyce yelled, closing her eyes. "The water will feel good if you manage to hit us."

Andy called down, "Who said it was water?"

Joyce and Sam bolted from their chairs and ran after the boys.

sunday morning, as everyone was scrambling to get ready for Sunday service, Gina walked into the apartment, dressed for church in a white eyelet sundress and carrying a matching purse. Uhmma and Apa paused midstep on their way to the kitchen. Andy looked up from his video game. Helen stopped clearing the breakfast plates. And Joyce put down the phone she had just picked up to call Gina.

"Gina!" Joyce yelped with joy and ran to her friend. Uhmma and Apa smiled. Andy waved as he looked down at his game again, and Helen simply nodded as she picked up the rest of the plates and headed over to the sink.

"We have to talk," Gina muttered and flicked her eyes toward Joyce's bedroom.

"I know," Joyce said and led the way back to her room.

After Joyce closed the door and then opened it quickly to make sure Andy wasn't snooping, Joyce pressed her back to the door and faced Gina.

"I'm so sorry—" Joyce started.

"We can talk about that later." Gina rushed to Joyce's side. "I just heard that John and his father are coming to church today."

Joyce's hands leaped to her eyes. "What! Today? Sunday, today?"

"Yes!" Gina said.

Joyce sank to the ground. "I can't do it," Joyce whispered. "I can't. I can't see him without my eyes."

Gina reached down and pulled Joyce back up. "Come on. We have some work to do."

Joyce stared at her friend. "What are you talking about?"

Gina removed her purse. "I've got you covered."

Joyce and Gina sat on the floor and studied the invisible double-sided tape that Gina had picked up from the Asian cosmetics lady at the department store.

"Arlene said that we can cut it with some scissors to match the crease."

"Are you sure it's going to work?" Joyce asked.

Gina shrugged. "Arlene said it should be a snap."

Joyce spontaneously reached over and embraced Gina in a hug. Tears sprang to Joyce's eyes. It was so good to have Gina back.

Gina patted Joyce's back. "Sam told me he talked to you."

Joyce pulled back and grinned at her friend. "I thought you only did the Godzilla imitation for me."

Gina lowered her eyes and tried not to smile. "Yeah, well, he's kind of special."

Joyce pumped her arms in the air. "I knew it!"

Gina rolled her eyes. "Okay, okay. Let's focus. We only have a half hour before church, and someone isn't even dressed."

Joyce glanced down at her pajamas. "We better get moving. Let me get my scissors." Joyce ran over to her bureau and began rummaging through the stuff that always magically collected there.

A sharp knock at the door was followed by Helen's head poking in. "Can I just get my clothes for church?"

Joyce waved her in. "Sure."

Helen stepped inside and headed over to the closet. Joyce pushed aside papers and keys and ponytail holders. "Helen, have you seen my scissors anywhere?"

"There's a pair inside my orange book bag," Helen said, pointing to her tropical bags in the corner.

"Thanks," Joyce said and started to cross the room to fetch the scissors. As she was passing Helen, Joyce gave her an imploring look and quickly cut her eyes to Gina, who was still sitting on the floor, assembling all the brushes and makeup for Joyce's makeover. It was important to Joyce that she clear the air with Gina. For as long as Joyce had been Gina's friend, they had shared everything with each other. She wanted Gina and Helen to know that Joyce trusted Gina completely.

Helen pressed her lips together for a moment and then threw her hands up in the air. Joyce mouthed silently, Thank you.

Helen nodded and pulled a dress and some shoes from the closet. Joyce found the scissors and brought them over to Gina. Before Helen left the room, she stood at the door for a moment. Joyce glanced up and saw the line of pain etched into her sister's forehead. Helen slowly turned away from the two best friends and left the room, closing the door behind her.

"I have to tell you something, Gina," Joyce said.

Gina raised up the piece of tape and held it near Joyce's eyes. "In a minute," Gina said. "Let's just do the hard part first and then we can talk while we work on your makeup."

"Okay," Joyce sighed and held still as Gina brought the tape closer.

"Darn," Gina said and lowered the crescent-moon-shaped piece of tape. "I have to cut it some more."

After several more tries and with tape stuck to every part of their hands, Gina carefully applied a thin sliver of tape to Joyce's right eyelid.

"Okay," Joyce said. "Dr. Reiner used his tweezers and kind of lifted part of my eyelid skin."

Gina grabbed her tweezers and zeroed in on Joyce's eyes.

"Whoa, cowboy," Joyce said and leaned back. "I still want my vision after you're done."

Gina raised one eyebrow and cleared her throat, the tweezers still raised in the air. Joyce slowly leaned forward. Gina gently grasped a bit of Joyce's upper eyelid skin and pulled it up.

"Is it working?" Joyce asked nervously, trying hard not to blink.

Gina stared at Joyce's eyes. "Hold on one second."

Gina positioned the tweezers at the outer edge of Joyce's eyes and pinched some skin.

"Ow, ow, ow, owwwww!" Joyce's voice grew louder in proportion to the pain.

Gina's eyes were crossed in concentration. "I almost have it. There." Gina took a deep breath and sat back.

Joyce reached up to the very edge of her eye, trying to massage the pinching pain away.

"Stop, Joyce," Gina said. "You'll ruin it."

Joyce lowered her hand. "That hurt."

Gina ignored her comment and went right on cutting the next sliver of tape for the other eye. Joyce dug through Gina's pile of makeup for a compact to check her eyelid.

"Wow!" Joyce exclaimed as she checked the fold in the mirror. "It looks perfect!"

Gina mumbled as she cut, "You always doubt me."

Joyce lowered the mirror. "No, I don't."

"Yes, you do."

Joyce opened her mouth to disagree again but then stopped. What was she fighting about? Gina was here, despite the way Joyce had acted on the beach, despite the fact that Joyce had not called all week to apologize. Gina was here to rescue Joyce. There was no question about it. Joyce reached over and touched Gina's elbow. Gina was here for Joyce.

"Sorry," Joyce said.

"It's okay," Gina said, her head still lowered in concentration as she carefully cut. "Ready for the next one?"

Joyce nodded.

Gina held up the tape. "Okay, you have to turn off the waterworks."

Joyce smiled and blinked back the tears.

"Better," Gina said and smiled.

After the second eyelid was taped back, Gina quickly worked on Joyce's makeup. As she was lightly dusting Joyce with some powder to set the eye shadow, Joyce tried to broach the subject of Helen.

"Hey, Gina," Joyce said, "I have to tell you something."

Gina flicked the brush across Joyce's forehead and then sat back.

"I have to tell you something, too," Gina said.

"Helen—"

"Sam—"

They both stopped.

"You go. I want to hear all about Sam," Joyce said.

Gina fiddled with her brush. "When Sam and I first started hanging out, he told me how he kind of had this crush on you."

"What?" Joyce exclaimed. "But he likes you."

Gina nodded. "That only happened after we had hung out this week and then I did the Godzilla line."

Joyce grinned. "You broke him with the Godzilla line. Man, I can't wait to tell that to your kids."

"Shut up." Gina laughed and threw the brush at Joyce. "It wasn't like that." Gina grew serious. "I didn't mean for him to stop liking you, but it wasn't as if you liked him that way and I needed someone to talk to who could understand. He was so nice about everything. I don't know. Everything started to change after I took him to the department store to get him some lip balm."

"Yeah," Joyce said. "He mentioned how impressed he was with your knowledge."

"Really?" Gina perked up. "What else did he say about me?"

Joyce wanted to stop time for a moment. To catch that shy happy smile on Gina's face. To savor the feeling of closeness. To memorize every passing second because next summer, after senior year, they weren't going to have all the time in the world to talk. They might even be clear across the country from each other.

"Joyce?"

Joyce blinked and turned to Gina. "He just said he thought you were wonderful."

Gina beamed. "He's pretty cool, too. Did he tell you about his skin?"

"Yeah," Joyce said.

"It's almost over," Gina said. "I had no idea the side effects could be so bad."

"What do you mean?"

"Like that day on the beach," Gina said. "He's not supposed to be in the sun for too long, but he wanted to finish up the project, and he got this killer headache afterwards."

"Didn't help that I was a bitch, either," Joyce muttered.

Gina didn't disagree. "Anyway, the side effects are mostly over now that he's tapering off of the medication." Gina opened up her lip gloss case and stared down at the little squares of various shades of red as she added, "His skin will clear up just in time for him to dump me when I get those nasty metal braces."

Joyce leaned forward. "You're getting braces?"

Gina shrugged. "Yeah. It's about time, and I don't

want to have them forever in college, which would be the kiss of death, right?" Gina glanced up, her face held tightly in place. "I finally have enough money saved up."

"I thought you wanted braces," Joyce said.

Gina stared up at the ceiling. "I do, I do, but I hate the thought of how ugly they are." Gina pointed at Joyce. "You said it yourself about Lynn, remember? How ugly her metal braces made her look."

"Yeah, but Lynn doesn't even look like you and—"

Gina shook her head. "They're going to look awful. I don't even know what colors to coordinate with gunmetal gray." Gina threw up her hands. "Seriously, what matches with ugly?" Gina waited a beat. "More ugly," she said and pointed a finger at herself.

"Gina, no. That's not true. You are not going to look ugly."

"Well, it doesn't matter. My teeth will get straight, and maybe my bucks will finally get into line," Gina said. "I just hope Sam sticks around, but knowing my luck, he'll take one look at my jaws of death and run the other direction."

Joyce patted Gina's back, trying to think of something to make her feel better, something to rescue her from her fate.

Someone knocked at the door. Joyce turned around as Andy poked his head in. "Uhmma says it's time to go."

"Okay," Joyce said.

Andy started to pull his head back and then stopped. "Black goes with everything," he said and quickly shut the door.

"Your lips," Gina said and held out her lip gloss brush.

Joyce turned back to Gina and let her apply the mauve color to her lips.

"What were you saying about Helen?" Gina asked.

"It's a long story. I'll tell you later."

"Okay," Gina said and leaned back to inspect her handiwork. "You look beautiful."

Joyce smiled without reaching for the compact to check Gina's work. "Thank you."

Gina and Joyce raced up the stairs leading from the parking lot to the church courtyard. A large group of people milled outside as they waited for their turn to enter the main hall. Gina and Joyce got into line and then immediately leaned out to see past the bodies.

"I don't see him anywhere," Gina said, craning her head.

"It's no use. How are we supposed to find him in this crowd?" Joyce said, gnawing in frustration at the webbing of skin on her hand.

"Joyce, stop chewing on your skin," Gomo said, coming up behind them along with the rest of Joyce's family.

Joyce reluctantly pulled her hand away from her face and greeted Gomo with a kiss. "On-young-ha-say-yo, Gomo. You look very nice today. That blouse goes well with your lipstick."

Gina turned around and waved. "Hi, Gomo."

Gomo did her best to smile back. "You two are looking especially pretty for church today. I like that both of you are wearing dresses instead of those pants for once."

"Thank you, Gomo," Joyce and Gina chirped.

Suddenly, Gina gripped Joyce's forearm. Out of the corner of her lips, Gina muttered, "Far right corner of the courtyard. White shirt, gray slacks, killer tan."

Joyce's eyes jumped at Gina's instructions. John Ford Kang was standing with his father near some bushes in the corner. His father was deep in conversation with another older gentleman while John stood there awkwardly, his hands fiddling with his striped tie.

Joyce tried not to crane her head as she peered over someone standing in front of her. John gazed in her direction just as Joyce jumped a little to get a better look at him.

"Ahhh," Joyce said and crouched down low. She didn't want him to think she was that desperate to see him.

"Joyce, stand up," Gomo instructed.

Joyce stood up straighter but put a hunch into her posture. "I think he saw me," Joyce whispered to Gina.

"Ohhhh, someone else spotted him, too," Gina reported.

Joyce had to peek again. She angled herself directly behind another man and then stole a quick glance. Lisa Yim was walking up to John's group. Lisa linked arms with the gentleman talking to John's father and talked animatedly to John.

Joyce slouched forward. "I have no chance with Lisa Yim around."

"What do you mean?" Gina asked, watching them.

"She told me that John likes her."

"No, he does not," Gina stated.

"Look at her. She's gorgeous. How do you know he doesn't like her?" Joyce wondered.

"Because I heard that he turned Lisa down when she asked him out."

Joyce gasped. "Are you sure?"

"Positive."

"Who's your source?"

Gina pointed at herself.

Joyce's eyes widened in disbelief.

"I work at a department store. A lot of people walk through there. I can't help it if I happen to overhear conversations about a certain high school student having the nerve to turn down a certain college student, while I'm crouched strategically in a nook behind all the gift bags, which are free after a purchase worth more than nineteen ninety-nine."

Joyce shook her head. "Sam was right. You are dangerous."

"What did Sam say?"

Joyce started to answer when she felt a tap on her shoulder.

"Hi, Joyce."

Joyce recognized the voice as though it were the sound of her beating heart. Instantly. There was a sudden hush of voices. Joyce slowly turned around. She felt like she was underwater, trying to move quickly only to find her limbs pushing against all that weight. The crowd of faces around her stretched and elongated, blending into the background as one face crystallized in front of her. John Ford Kang. Joyce blinked. He was still there.

"Hey," she said weakly and focused on making sure her knees wouldn't buckle.

"Hey. Can I stand in line with you?"

"Uh, sure," Joyce said. Gina ribbed her in the side. "Oh, this is my friend Gina."

John reached over and shook Gina's hand. "Hey, I remember you from AP Art History."

"Yeah, that's right." Gina's cheeks bunched up and she beamed out her best teeth-baring smile. It didn't take much to win over Gina.

John turned back to Joyce. "You didn't stay for the barbecue after the volleyball game."

"Oh, right. I had to work that night," Joyce squeaked.

"But not as much now, right? Especially with that new waitress," John said.

Joyce stared at him. Had he been by the restaurant again?

The line started to move forward. As they stepped toward the entrance to the church, Gina poked Joyce in the side and pointed her chin in someone's direction. Joyce glanced over to find Lisa Yim standing near the entrance, squinting in her direction. Her eyes narrowed into focused lasers on Joyce and her family as John walked beside them. Just as they entered the church, Joyce saw Lisa rushing off into the fellowship hall, her cell phone pressed firmly to her ear as her entourage of girlfriends swarmed around her.

John sat with his father a few rows down from them. Joyce tried not to stare at the back of his head the whole time, but after a minute of counting light fixtures, Joyce let her eyes wander back over. It just killed her the way his hair curled at the edges like that. Must be from all the seawater, Joyce reasoned.

At the end of the sermon, as Joyce tried to nonchalantly take her time getting out of her row, Gomo took her hand and led her past the line of people waiting to shake the pastor's hand and out into the courtyard.

"Joyce," Gomo said, "I did not have time to tell you earlier, but the surgery is next week."

"Next week? I thought it was next month."

"Dr. Rie-ne-or's office called and said they could fit you in sooner."

"But next week, my friend is having a show." Joyce groaned and threw back her head, her eyes shut tight against the thought of trying to explain to Gina and Sam.

"I have already made the appointment," Gomo said. "I am sure your friend will understand."

Joyce nodded and turned to leave.

"The handsome boy is over in the fellowship hall with his father," Gomo said and walked away.

Joyce wandered into the fellowship hall, where Uhmma and some of the other mothers were setting out the food. John was with his father getting coffee. Joyce stood in the doorway, wondering if she should go over and talk to him. Would it be obvious that Joyce was following him around? Where was Gina? Joyce checked the crowd. No Gina or Sam. Joyce was on her own this time, but she could handle this. She could face John Ford Kang because she was ready. Joyce flipped her hair off her shoulders. Check. She ran her finger along the edge of her lips to erase any lipstick smudges. Check. She gingerly reached up to check her eyes. Sticky tape. Joyce quickly turned around and bolted from the room. As she ran for the bathroom, her gaze firmly on the ground, she reached up to her upper eyelids again. Her eyelids had fallen.

Joyce made it into the bathroom without anyone stopping her. Three stalls were full, so she headed to the farthest stall to wait them out. Two toilets flushed almost at the same time. Joyce could hear the water running as the women chatted and washed their hands. Just before they were about to leave, the third toilet flushed and the sound of sharp metal heel taps echoed through the bathroom.

"Hi, Lisa," one voice called out.

Shushed conversation slipped back and forth. Then suddenly a voice rang out in alarm, "Helen Kim. Gay!"

"Shhhh!"

The women switched to Korean, but continued to whisper urgently as they headed out the door. Joyce sat completely frozen. Had she really heard what she thought she had heard? Shoot. Joyce slammed the side of her head with the heel of her hand. Why hadn't she checked their shoes? Who were those women that Lisa had been talking to? Joyce recalled Lisa saying how Su Yon's mother and Lisa's mother had grown up in the same village. Joyce knew Lisa was kind of superficial, but to be so vicious and cruel—that over-inflated weasel of a gossip. Joyce wanted to pop those balloons she called breasts and watch them leak and sag to Lisa's knees. Joyce slammed her fist into the stall door and stepped out.

This was going to kill Helen. Joyce had to warn her. News like this spread quicker than a virus. As Joyce quickly turned to leave, her reflection in the mirror caught her eyes. Joyce groaned. She forgot she had to reattach her eyelids. It would take forever without Gina to help her. Joyce stepped closer to the mirror. She couldn't face John without the folds. And if she didn't make her impression today, Lisa Yim would just swoop right in. What should she do? She didn't have enough time. Joyce started at herself and exhaled slowly. There was only one true answer. Joyce pulled the tape off her skin.

"Owww!" Joyce yelled. God, beauty hurt.

Joyce flew out of the bathroom and raced into the courtyard. Small groups were gathered together in conversation. Some people's eyes turned in her direction when she stepped onto the shaded area. Joyce found herself studying everyone's lips, looking for words like *Helen* and *gay*. She frantically scoured the yard for Helen. On a far bench, Sam and Gina sat talking and laughing. Joyce rushed over.

"Hey," Joyce said breathlessly, "have you seen Helen?"

Gina turned to her with a smile until she saw Joyce's face. "Joyce, what happened to your eyes?"

"They fell. I'll explain later," Joyce said.

"Joyce, we can fix them. I have more tape," Gina said, standing up.

"It doesn't matter anymore. You have to help me find Helen."

"Joyce," Gina said, "calm down. What's going on? Is something wrong with Helen?"

Joyce bit her bottom lip, trying to contain all the thoughts jamming into her mind. Everywhere she looked, more and more faces seemed to be glancing in Joyce's direction, lips whispering. The news was spreading.

"I need to find Helen," Joyce said.

Gina stood up in alarm. "Okay, Joyce. Let's go."

Sam stood up as well, and the three of them walked from area to area, combing the faces for Helen. Joyce continued to see the looks, hear the whispers, as she passed. With each glance, Joyce stood up straighter. With every conversation that suddenly hushed as she approached, she added a swing to her hips. Who did these people think they were to talk about Helen like she had a disease or something? Joyce walked through the church like she owned the place.

As she stepped inside the fellowship hall, Joyce froze as soon as she saw John standing near the door, eating a chocolate doughnut. Somehow the sight of him and chocolate together was just enough to make Joyce stumble and crumble to the ground. Gina caught her right before her ass hit the floor.

John rushed over. "Whoa. Are you okay?" He took her hand and helped her up.

Joyce immediately felt her face flush red. "I'm such a klutz," she said.

John smiled. "I seem to inspire that reaction in you."

"Huh?" Joyce said.

"You're always falling down when you see me."

Joyce groaned and laughed. John smiled down at her and in that moment, she realized that John didn't even notice that anything was different about her. And without the folds, Joyce felt like herself around him instead of some coy cheerleader-type character.

"Can I get you a doughnut?" John offered.

Joyce stared into his eyes for a second. This had to be dream. "No, I'm okay," she said.

"Joyce," Gina called out, "Helen is in the kitchen."

Joyce refocused her attention. "I'll catch you later," she said and stepped away from John.

John pointed his finger at her. "No. I'll catch you later. That's a promise."

Joyce walked away with a shake of her head. He was kind of a dork. Joyce smiled. She could really fall for him.

Helen was in the kitchen with Uhmma and a few of the other women, cleaning up the dishes. Joyce raced over to her and muttered urgently, "We have to talk."

Helen continued drying a dish. "What's up, Joyce?"

"Privately," Joyce said.

Helen tilted her head but handed Uhmma the dish before following Joyce to the back of the kitchen.

"I heard some women talking about you," Joyce whispered.

"What do you mean?" Helen said, her eyes on the floor.

"They said your name and then *gay*."

Helen covered her mouth with her hand. After a moment, she raised her eyes and fired off angrily, "Damn it, Joyce. I knew Gina would talk."

Joyce stepped back. "Helen," Joyce started to explain.

"That blabbermouth friend of yours," Helen said, her jaw clenching and unclenching.

"Helen, I never got the chance to tell Gina. It wasn't her."

Helen's eyes wrinkled in confusion. "Then who was it? I don't understand who would want to spread that news about me. Are you sure you heard correctly?"

Joyce nodded. She could tell Helen about Lisa and John later.

Helen turned away. Uhmma saw the look on Helen's face and left the two ladies she was speaking with and came over to them.

"What is wrong, Helen?" Uhmma asked.

"Joyce said she heard some women talking about me in the bathroom."

Uhmma touched Helen's face. "What do you want to do?"

"I just want to go home. I don't want to deal with this here, now."

Uhmma quickly shed the apron and waved good-bye to the women.

The three of them stepped out into the fellowship hall, and this time Joyce knew for sure that she was not imagining things. Almost every pair of eyes turned and glanced over at them. Uhmma reached out and grasped each daughter's hand and with her head perfectly poised, walked them through the hall and out into the courtyard.

Gomo was sitting with some of her older lady friends and as soon as she saw Uhmma with Helen and Joyce, she stood up. Her friends glanced from Gomo to Uhmma and then back to Gomo. Uhmma paused for a second in her step, but then she strode forward. Gomo blocked Uhmma's path.

Gomo whispered, "If you had made Helen keep dating Mr. Moon, we would not have to face these ugly rumors."

Uhmma turned to Gomo, her face calm and for once unconcerned with anything Gomo had said. "They are not rumors."

Gomo's eyes widened in shock.

"Please, Gomo, I will explain everything back at home. This is not the place to have such an important conversation. Our family is what matters the most right now. You have always said this, and it is still true. We are a family, and we must support and help one another."

Gomo lowered her eyes. Uhmma waited, her eyes softening as Gomo struggled to compose herself. Even though half of Gomo's face was frozen, even Joyce could see the lines of pain wrinkling the few areas that could move.

Apa and Andy came rushing over from the far

playground near the parking lot, with Sam right behind them.

"Yuh-boh," Apa said, "is everything all right?"

Uhmma nodded tightly and then glanced at Gomo, who was standing off to the side, clutching her purse, immobile and mute, while her eyes darted from family member to family member.

Sam walked up and stood near Gina, who glanced at him with a grateful smile. Mrs. Lee, when she noticed her friends and daughter gathered together, stopped conversing with the pastor's wife and walked over to them. The entire family gathered together in a tight circle around Helen. Joyce could feel Helen's body trembling next to her, so she reached out and took Helen's hand. All around them the congregation continued to ripple with whispers while they stood silently in the eye of the storm. Helen kept her head up, refusing to let anyone see her upset. Joyce glanced over at a small circle of people standing on the lawn laughing especially loud. Lisa Yim and her friends. Joyce found herself longing for a dart to aim at Lisa's chest. Andy caught her gaze and narrowed his eyes at Lisa.

"Let us go," Uhmma said quietly and began to move forward. The group followed her lead and headed for the stairs that led down to the parking lot. Gomo stepped forward and joined the family, gesturing to her friends to follow. The older ladies fell into step behind Gomo. Some people called out their good-byes as the family slowly exited the courtyard. Others reached out and shook Apa's hand or bowed to Gomo and the elder ladies.

John and his father were standing off to the side watching everything unfold with puzzled looks on their faces. It had definitely been a while since they had experienced a Sunday at the Korean church. As Joyce passed John, she peeked over at him and caught his eyes. John raised two fingers in a peace sign and winked.

This time, Joyce winked back.

Just as everyone was heading down the steps, Andy broke from the group, running quickly across the lawn. He did a commando tumble-roll move and then aimed his squirt gun right at Lisa Yim. He fired off two rounds of some syrupy substance that clung and slowly dripped down the front of her dress. Bull's-eye.

Lisa stared down at her chest and began to scream. Andy took off running and joined the family again.

"What's in there?" Joyce asked, half hoping he wouldn't tell her, since she had almost been sprayed by the same stuff just the other day.

"I crushed all my shark liver extract pills and loaded them into my gun," Andy said. "I was saving it for Tom Koh, but he was sick today."

"You are so gross," Joyce said with a grin. "Good aim."

Andy pointed at himself. "And Uhmma thought those video games would just rot my brain."

joyce sat in Dr. Reiner's outpatient operating room, the crinkle of her paper gown as loud as the boom of her heartbeat in her ears. This was it. The final moment before she would enter her cocoon to emerge as a gorgeous new butterfly. Joyce worried the front of her gown as she waited for Dr. Reiner to enter. To keep her mind off the imminent procedure, she tried to imagine what Gina was doing right then. Probably shopping for a new dress to wear to the opening of Sam's show the next day. Joyce stared up at the lights and started counting all the fixtures. Gina was out there having fun while Joyce sat here waiting to get cut up. The thought of sitting around at home the next few days, woozy on painkillers, did not seem very glamorous.

Joyce swung her legs and took deep breaths through her mouth to quell the nausea that arose instantly at the thought of all that pain. She tried to imagine what Helen was doing. Packing. Helen was probably getting all her books and clothes together to move into the dorms. Joyce smiled at the thought of Helen's face glowing with anticipation. For the first time, Helen was going to have a life of her own. It had been a long time since Joyce remembered seeing her sister so happy. And for the first time in her whole life, Joyce was going to have her own room.

Darn! Joyce punched the padded bed she was sitting on. She was going to miss out on the shopping sprees Gomo had promised to help decorate Helen's and Joyce's new rooms. She knew Gomo would take her after she was well enough to go out, but shopping with Helen and Gomo would have been much more enjoyable. Argh!

It would only be a few weeks of recuperation, but even that time seemed endless compared to all that Joyce would be missing and had missed while she had been so preoccupied with the way she looked. The longer she sat there waiting, the more it felt like life was moving forward without her. Joyce bit her lower lip. And what if John called? How was she going to explain why she couldn't see him for a while? He would show up at church and she wouldn't be there to talk to him. But Lisa Yim would be there for sure. Joyce stared pinching the fat above her knees. That Lisa Yim would use every trick she knew to get John.

Joyce sighed. What was taking so long? She jumped off the bed and started to pace. What was she doing here waiting anyway? Was this what she really wanted? She had believed the folds would make her more attractive and confident, but it was feeling more and more like an obstacle to all the things that she really wanted to be doing. Who was this girl, woman, young adult sitting here waiting to change? Did this define her? And if she didn't really know herself, know what was true to her, then how could she begin to permanently change her face? Would she regret it later? Joyce didn't know. And that was a problem.

Joyce stood up and grabbed the back of her gown to keep her butt covered up and stepped out into the hall.

"Excuse me," she called out. "Excuse me."

Gomo and Uhmma were looking at magazines when Joyce walked out into the waiting room, dressed in her regular clothes.

Uhmma stood up and rushed to her side. "Did something go wrong, Joyce?"

Gomo dropped her magazine on the coffee table. "She could not do it."

Joyce shook her head. "I don't want my eyes to look any different. I don't care about getting a san-gah-pu-rhee. I thought it was what I wanted to help me look better and feel good about myself, but I'm tired of being obsessed with how I look. I'm okay with being just me. And I have a lot of other things I want to do this summer."

Uhmma nodded.

Gomo stepped forward. "Would you like me to reschedule Dr. Rie-ne-or? Maybe this is not the best time for you."

Joyce bowed to Gomo and said, "Gam-sah-ham-nee-da, Gomo. I appreciate your offer, but this is who I am." Joyce looked down at herself. "I might not be the prettiest or the smartest or even know what I want to be someday, but I do know what's important to me right now." Joyce paused, nervously glancing at Uhmma before asking Gomo a question. "I have a request, Gomo. Instead of paying for me to get my eyes done, can you use the money to help Gina get clear braces for her teeth instead?"

Gomo tilted her head in confusion. "You want me to help Gina with her braces?"

Uhmma's eyes softened as she studied her younger daughter's face.

Joyce nodded. "It would make Gina's year."

Gomo thought it over. "I see no problem with that."

Uhmma smiled at Joyce. "Mrs. Lee will be very happy for the help."

Gomo reached out and patted Joyce's shoulders. "You are just like me. Such a big heart."

Joyce grinned. It wasn't so bad to be like Michael, after all. Besides, if Joyce ever wanted the folds back in her eyes, she had some glue that Dr. Reiner had happily provided for her. Joyce reached behind her and patted the bump in her back pocket. Who knew when she might need a shot of adventure? There was no harm in having a little fun.